The House of Hale Book Three

The Earl and the Heir

By

GL Robinson

Cover art by Bart Lindstrom. Used with grateful thanks by permission of the artist.

For more information on this wonderful artist go to:

http://www.bartlindstrom.com/

As always, in memory of my dear sister
Francine
And with thanks
To my ARC Readers, who tell me what to do
And Thomas E. Burch for his patient technical help

A note to my readers:

I realize, belatedly, that I suffer from Transcontinental Spelling Disease. That is to say, sometimes I use British spelling and sometimes American. I hope it doesn't impair your enjoyment of my stories and that in a weird way it helps to bring our two cultures together.
For more information about me (and why I have international spelling!), to listen to me read from my books, receive a free short story, or get sneak previews about upcoming books, please go to:

https://romancenovelsbyglrobinson.com

© GL Robinson 2020. All Rights Reserved.

Table of Contents

CHAPTER ONE 1
CHAPTER TWO 6
CHAPTER THREE 17
CHAPTER FOUR 29
CHAPTER FIVE 38
CHAPTER SIX 49
CHAPTER SEVEN 59
CHAPTER EIGHT 67
CHAPTER NINE 76
CHAPTER TEN 87
CHAPTER ELEVEN 97
CHAPTER TWELVE 107
CHAPTER THIRTEEN 115
CHAPTER FOURTEEN 124
CHAPTER FIFTEEN 133
CHAPTER SIXTEEN 141
CHAPTER SEVENTEEN 157
CHAPTER EIGHTEEN 173
CHAPTER NINETEEN 183
CHAPTER TWENTY 199
CHAPTER TWENTY-ONE 206
CHAPTER TWENTY-TWO 217
About the Author 232

CHAPTER ONE

In which Lord Hale returns from the country

"Papa! Papa!" Sylvester Barrington, aged three years and two months, heir and hope of the House of Hale heard his Sire's voice in the hall. He leaped down from the table where he sat painting with his Mama, oblivious to the overturned jar of paint water that tumbled in his wake, and ran towards the hall, his half-unbuttoned nankeens falling from his long-legged little person.

"What's this? Why are you appearing in this disheveled state, Sirrah? Don't you know a gentleman never unbuttons his pantaloons in public?"

So saying, the Earl caught his son up in his arms and kissed him soundly on his sticky cheek. "Where's your poor Mama? Have you been causing her unholy distress?"

"No, I not 'stress, Papa, I bin paintin'," responded the young lord, rubbing his curly head on his father's coat.

"So I see," answered his father, coming into the living room with his son in his arms and observing the muddy flood that had now reached the carpet. "Go and ask Pennyworth to send someone to clean up your painting."

He put his son down and strode over to his wife Sophy who had been trying to stem the flow, and now turned to greet him. He took her in a crushing embrace and kissed her long and lovingly.

When at last they broke apart, he said, "I am gone under two weeks, my love, and our son has apparently already fallen into the habits of his father, regarding women and muddy water!"

"If you are referring to the circumstances of our meeting, when you splashed me with a ditch full of mud because you were cross and not paying attention to your horses, I can only say that you are mistaken," retorted his wife. "Your son spilled the water because he loves you above all things, even trifle. He has been waiting these last four hours for you to arrive. He heard your voice and leaped."

"Even trifle, eh? I dare say it won't last. The first time I refuse him something he has set his mind on, he will revert to the trifle. But I am more constant. I shall always love *you* more than trifle." He kissed her on the cheek. "More than roast beef." He kissed her below her ear. "More than *Fino*." He kissed her throat.

Since her husband had just mentioned his three favorite comestibles, Sophy was suitably impressed, but before she could respond with an appropriate show of appreciation, two maids came in. One was bearing a mop and bucket, and the other was being pulled along by the young lord, who was telling her seriously,

"My Papa comed home. His name is 'Sander. His Papa's name 'Vester and my name 'Vester too."

The maid, who had only come up from the country the week before, was wearing the dark blue dress and apron that denoted her as a kitchen maid. She had never been above stairs before and certainly never even thought of his lordship as having a first name. She shrank away towards the door, but young Sylvester was having none of it.

"Come on Daisy! Don't be 'fraid! He's nice. He let you eat his tifle."

Her ladyship came forward, smiling. "Come in... Daisy, is it? I hope Sylvester isn't keeping you from your work. He is very demanding, I know."

"Oh no, me lady, me lord," Daisy bobbed a curtsey to each of them. "It's me what looked after the little 'uns at home till I was old enough to leave. I liked playing with 'em, but I didn't let them get away with nuffin. They minded me."

"Excellent!" said his lordship. "If you can get my son to mind you it will be more than anyone else has been able to do! Thank you, Daisy. Let her go now, Sylvester. She has work to do."

"I work too," said the young lord stoutly. "I help, can't I, Papa?" He gazed up at his father with the wide blue eyes of his mother.

The Earl looked at his wife who said, "Well, that depends on Daisy. You must be honest with us, Daisy. Is he getting under your feet?"

"Oh no, me lady," said the maid. "He is a lovely little man, and he teaches me to talk proper."

"Good God," muttered his lordship.

"Very well then," said the anxious mother, "but you must send him away if he prevents you from carrying out your duties. If he's still below stairs at six o'clock, please ask Mrs. Green to give him his supper." She knelt down to look in her son's face. "Sylvester, if Daisy tells you to come above stairs, you must come to find Papa and me. Please be a gentleman and do not argue! Promise!"

"I pomise!" declared the young lord.

By now the puddle had been mopped up. Both maids curtseyed and left, Sylvester holding Daisy's hand and still talking.

"See, Daisy! I tole you my Papa is nice. My Mama nice too, only she doesn't give you her tifle." His voice grew fainter.

"I don't give him my trifle?" exclaimed Sophy. "That's because between the pair of you, there's never any left!" She turned to her husband, "What are we going to do with him? They can't keep entertaining him below stairs. If only you wouldn't keep dismissing the nannies!"

"If only they wouldn't keep trying to prevent him from doing what is reasonable for a boy to do, and instead turn him into some sort of puppet. That last one put him in the corner without his supper because his curls were in disorder! He had only tried standing on his head and they fell in his face."

"Oh, Lysander! You know they fell in his face because when he tried standing on his head, he tangled the tablecloth in his boots and pulled everything on top of himself. It's lucky he wasn't hurt."

"If the silly woman had held his feet, he would never have fallen. What do you expect a boy to do? Sit and read the Bible? That's what she wanted, evidently."

"I know a certain grown-up boy who sits and reads Marcus Aurelius and Ovid," said Sophy fondly, referring to her husband's frequent reading matter. She kissed him and looking meaningfully into his eyes said, "Anyway, why are we wasting time down here talking when we could be... upstairs. After all, we have to change for dinner and you're still in your riding boots. Sylvester appears to be busy and we could..." She did not finish her sentence.

His lordship raised one eyebrow. "Are you propositioning me, Lady Hale?" he said.

"Yes," she replied, "and I expect my curls to be *very* disordered."

She walked briskly towards the stairs.

CHAPTER TWO

In which his lordship engages a nursemaid

Lady Hale went into her bedchamber, took off her gown and petticoat and then, clad only in her chemise, took the pins out of her hair and shook out her curls. His lordship came in moments later and watched his wife. The light from the candles on her dressing table flamed in the chestnut brown of the abundant hair he loved to see over her shoulders. It reminded him of when they first met. She had been drenched by his curricle and had let her hair down to dry. She had emerged in an old red gown, very low cut, flushed from the kitchen, with her wild curls covering the tops of her glorious breasts. He had loved her from that moment.

He went to her now and, lifting the hair from the back of her neck, kissed her there. Her body had returned to its normal size after the birth of their son and, holding her now, her husband marveled that the boy terrorizing the household downstairs could ever have emerged from her slim frame.

Sophy gave another murmur of pleasure and said, "We have to be quick, Lysander. I must put Sylvester to bed before dinner and it's already gone six."

His lordship groaned. "Are we never to have a moment's peace? God knows, I love my son, but you'd think in this whole household of people there would be someone to put him to bed so that you and I may be private together!"

He picked her up and carried her to the bed, which was still the bower painted with roses and cherubs they had come so near to breaking to pieces when they were first married. Lysander had been in favor of replacing it with a solid piece of English oak from Hale Court, their estate in the country, where the Earl had just spent ten days overlooking the spring planting. But Sophy loved the impractical French painted confection that matched the rest of her room, so it had been subject to repeated repairs.

Later, as they lay quiet, their breathing returning to normal, they heard the sound of small feet running along the hall. "Papa! Mama!" cried a familiar peremptory little voice. "Where you?"

"Don't answer," growled his lordship. "Perhaps he won't find us."

They heard the door of Lysander's room being opened and "Papa!" again, and then the communicating door between the bedchambers was flung open and a small figure marched into the room.

"Mama! Papa!" he began, then, seeing them in bed and obviously unclothed, he continued suspiciously, "Why you got no clothes on and why you in bed? 'Snot bedtime!"

"Er…" began his lordship, "er… we were tired and decided to lie down … but then we were very hot, so we took off our clothes. Anyway, young man, don't you know better than to come into your Mama's bedchamber like that, without knocking and waiting to be given leave to enter? Where are your manners? Is that what a gentleman would do?"

"No, Papa. But it's 'portant! Cook says..."

But his Papa did not give him time to finish. "Go outside again, knock on the door and wait to be admitted."

"But Papa, Cook says..."

"I don't care what Cook says. Do as I say!" The tone of his voice brooked no argument.

The young lord turned unwillingly and stamped out of the room.

"Close the door!" called his father.

They saw the door being closed. His lordship sprang out of bed and was pulling on his britches when they heard a knock and the door began to open.

"Did Mama say 'Come in'?" called Lysander, ruthlessly. "Close the door and wait until she says you may enter."

"But Papa! I did knocked! And Cook says..."

"I will not say it again. I do not care about Cook. Learn some manners or you will go to bed directly!"

"Oh, Lysander, let him in," said the devoted Mama. "You are almost dressed."

"No, let him learn some decorum. Good God! I never saw my father naked in my life and I certainly never saw my parents in bed together!"

"Perhaps, but you are not so stuffy!" responded his wife, smiling at him. "Why don't you go into your own room. I have to get dressed for dinner." And she called, "You may come in, Sylvester!"

Their son came in, a mulish look on his face. "*Now* I tell you 'bout Cook?" he asked angrily.

"If you control your temper and first say to Mama, 'Forgive my bad manners, Mama. I shall not do it again'," replied his father evenly but with a look in his eye that his son knew not to ignore.

"'Give my bad manners, Mama. I not do it gain."

"You are forgiven, my darling. Now, what did Cook say?"

Relieved that he could at last impart this critical information, Sylvester gave the lovely smile that was the image of his father's and answered, "Cook says she don't give me no tifle coz it's a new one an' she don't want to touch it till 'is lordship 'as some." He parroted the words as he had heard them.

His parents looked at each other. "You must say 'she *doesn't* want to touch it till *h*is lordship *h*as some'," corrected his mother gently. Papa and I say things one way and Cook... and Daisy," she added as an afterthought, "say them another way. Papa and I say *doesn't* not *don't* and *h*is not *'is*, and you want to be like Papa, don't you?"

Since his Papa was the light of his life, even more, as his Mama had observed, than trifle, the young lord wanted to be like him in every respect, so he replied reverently, "Yes!"

"Go and help Winton get Papa changed, then. I'm sure he'll talk to Cook about the trifle," said her ladyship. "I have to get dressed for dinner. Lysander, ring the bell for Susan, will you, before you go?"

The Earl and his heir went together into the next room where Sylvester peppered both him and his valet Winton with endless questions while his lordship dressed. Luckily,

Winton was used to it as there had been frequent periods between nannies, like this one, and the young master stayed glued to his father as much as he could.

"Why you tooken off your britches for washing?" he demanded as his Papa performed his ablutions behind the wash stand screen.

"A gentleman always washes before dinner, particularly here, you see," responded the Earl, demonstrating. "Remember that, Sylvester. A gentleman is always clean in his person."

"I not clean 'n my person," said his son, looking down at his very grubby nankeens which showed clear evidence of not only the painting exercise but also remnants of his dinner and something else his lordship could not define. Then remembering, he added, "I help Daisy with the wood for the fires!" It was one of the scullery maid's duties to fill the hods with logs for the upstairs maids to feed the fires. "Papa! There's a 'normous pile of wood downstairs an… an there's a mouse! I sawed it but I couldn't catched it! But Daisy said it's dirty! I dirty too, but Daisy said it all come out in the wash. Daisy said…"

"Daisy appears to have said a lot of very sensible things," reflected his lordship. "I wonder…" His voice trailed off.

But the young lord was on to something else. "Why you spit on my Papa's boots?" he demanded of Winton. "I want to spit too." And he spat, not very accurately, in the direction of his father's Hoby's.

"To get off the finger marks, you see," responded Winton, wiping the spit from his hand. "You don't want finger marks on your boots, young master."

Next came the excitement of pulling the boots on his father's long legs. Sylvester participated with more energy than skill, resulting in more spitting to remove fingerprints.

"That's entirely enough," said his lordship finally. "Come on. Let's go and see Cook about the trifle." He swung his son up onto his shoulders and ran him bouncing downstairs into the hall and then down the kitchen stairs in the back of the house. Sylvester squealed in delight as his father pretended to drop him on the kitchen floor, then finally set him down.

"'Gain! 'Gain!" he cried, but his father said, "Let me talk to Mrs. Green and you go and find Daisy." To the Cook he said, "Where's this wonderful trifle?"

When Mrs. Green brought it from the pantry, he looked at it and said, "It looks perfect and I know you don't want to spoil its beautiful symmetry, but please let the boy have some. I shall not mind if it's missing a portion when I see it later."

"As you wish, me lord," said the Cook, bobbing a curtsey. "I knows he do love his trifle. Just like you, me lord!"

"Indeed, Mrs. Green," replied his lordship with the charming smile he and his son had in common. "Indeed I do!"

Sylvester arrived, towing Daisy.

"Daisy," said his lordship, "if I have the agreement of Mrs. Wilkins, would you be nursemaid to this young hellion?" The maid looked a little perplexed. "To this young man," he amended. "It would mean spending a good deal of the day above stairs in the nursery and sleeping up there, too. But I don't mind his coming down here from time to time, especially for meals, if the rest of the staff can stand it. I don't see why food should be carried up and down for him."

His lordship remembered how, in his own youth, he had loved being able to escape to the kitchen, or the stables in the mews, or anywhere else he was not supposed to be. "And you must take him for walks, or, more probably, runs in the park. He needs to be outside as much as possible. You may use a carriage to get there."

"You mean, would I look after the young master, me lord?" asked Daisy in wonder. "Wouldn't I just! I miss the young 'uns at 'ome."

"Yes. It's not a job for the faint of heart… you have to be firm with him, I mean. But if you explain why things have to be, instead of just telling him what to do, he will mind you."

"Oh, he'll mind me, don't you fear, me lord," replied Daisy stoutly. "We gets along well, don't we, my young lord?"

"Just call him Sylvester. He'll get enough of this 'my lord' stuff when he's older. Let me go and talk to Mrs. Wilkins."

The object of their conversation had by now seen that the trifle was being served into a dish, a fact which had his whole attention. Daisy firmly admonished him to sit up properly at the table and use his spoon, and not his put his face into the dish.

Mrs. Wilkins, the housekeeper, was astonished when, after a knock at her door, his lordship came into her office. It was seldom that he had been there, on rare occasions sending her messages via Pennyworth. By contrast, her ladyship often came down to her rather than summoning her upstairs, even though the housekeeper had often protested that she would gladly come up. She stood and curtseyed.

"Please sit down, Mrs. Wilkins." He came straight to the point. "You probably know that we have had a good deal of difficulty in the matter of nannies for Sylvester."

She nodded, recalling the parade of women who had come and gone over the months, most of them unregretted. The position of nannies was always unenviable. They were not part of the downstairs staff, nor were they part of the upstairs family. They were conscious of their superiority over the servants but equally conscious that they were paid employees. This tended to make them haughty to the one and obsequious to the other.

"Well," he continued, "I propose to dispense with nannies altogether. I'd like the young maid Daisy to take over the position of nursemaid to the boy. She seems to have a good deal of experience with children at home and appears to be able to manage him. What's more, he likes her. I hope that won't interrupt your downstairs management too greatly?"

"If you think she would be suitable, my lord, I daresay we can manage downstairs without her. If not, we can see if another young person would wish to come from Hale Court. But she is very young and poorly educated. I doubt she would be able to teach him his letters or his numbers."

"Her ladyship or I can see to that. I am not looking for a tutor. That can wait a year or two. I want a person young enough to play with him but old enough to keep him out of scrapes. I have some confidence that she would do that. She cannot be worse than the dreadful matrons we have seen over the last two years. I wish to give it a try."

Hearing the finality in his lordship's tone, the housekeeper knew that the consultation, such as it was, was over.

"As you wish, my lord. I will talk to her about her new duties. It will mean a change in her remuneration, of course, and she will need new uniforms."

"I have already talked to her about her duties, but the rest I leave to you. She will take Sylvester upstairs now for his bath. He sorely needs one!"

Mrs. Wilkins curtseyed to the Earl, and he returned to the kitchen. There he found his son finishing the trifle and asking for more.

He was pleased to hear Daisy say,

"Think a minute, Sylvester. Your Papa 'asn't had 'is dinner yet and 'e will be wanting trifle too. You don't want to make him sad by eatin' it all, do you?"

Since his Papa was higher than God, the answer to this was obvious, and the boy submitted to getting down from the table. Calling for bathwater to be taken up to the nursery rooms, his lordship led both Daisy and his son upstairs. He told Sylvester that his Mama and Papa would return once he was in bed, and went down to meet his wife.

Sophy and Lysander enjoyed nearly an hour of uninterrupted time together discussing the latest on-dits in London and developments at Hale Court in Buckinghamshire. Then they both returned to the nursery and found their son and heir miraculously clean and tucked in his bed, complaining to Daisy.

"My Papa gived me a sword but I killed Nanny Smith with it and she made it go 'way. She said swords was silly, but my Papa gived me it and 'snot silly!"

He was referring to a wooden toy Lysander had played with when he was a child and which he had brought back from the Court on a previous trip.

"Swords isn't silly," commented Daisy, "but sometimes them using 'em is silly. Praps we can make a shape of a man for you to fight with, if I can find the sword Nanny hid. But you mustn't kill real people. Your Papa wouldn't like that, I'm sure."

"No, I most certainly wouldn't, thank you Daisy," announced his lordship, coming into the room. "Go downstairs now and see Mrs. Wilkins. She wishes to talk to you. We will stay here until Sylvester is asleep. Eat your own supper and come back when you can."

Her ladyship knelt by the bed with her son for his prayer. They recited together:

> *Matthew, Mark, Luke and John,*
> *Bless the bed that I lie on.*
> *Four corners to my bed,*

Four angels round my head.
A life that's full of naught but joy
And make of me a very good boy.

Then, as customary, Sylvester added, "God Bless Mama and Papa," and since they were uppermost in his mind this day "… and Daisy… and the mouse I didn't catched. Amen."

His Mama kissed him goodnight and sat off to one side while her husband settled him. He talked to him quietly, sitting on his bed, telling him about his visit to the Court: the stables, the animals, the fields, the farms, the people that would someday be his to manage. His gentle tone soon had its effect and Sylvester's eyes sank to half-closed, then closed. His father kissed his curly head and stood up. He went to his wife and the two of them stood, as parents have always done, looking at their offspring and wondering how such an angel could also be such an imp.

Daisy returned presently. "If you please, me lady," she whispered, bobbing a curtsey, "Mrs. Wilkins says can you see 'er tomorrow when convenient to talk about my uniform and other things."

Her ladyship nodded, and arm in arm, she and her husband went down to dinner.

CHAPTER THREE

In which Charles Alverstoke pays a visit

"I don't know any other father of our acquaintance," said Sophy, "who would arrange a nursemaid for his son. You really are the most *managing* of men. I suppose I should be used to it by now, but I don't know whether to be grateful or affronted. I could have done it myself, you know."

"Of course you could," responded her husband, "but now you don't have to. You can put all your energies into looking after me. I have been most dreadfully neglected of late."

"Lysander! What stuff! You've been from home for over two weeks! I couldn't have *looked after* you if I had wanted to!"

"I'm a pitiful object of neglect," said her husband with a downcast air that looked so like their son in a fit of sulks that Sophy laughed.

"It's no laughing matter!" objected her husband. "You must start looking after me immediately or I may fall into a decline."

Since anyone less in a decline than her tall, handsome husband could scarcely be imagined, Sophy laughed even more.

This conversation took place after the couple had retired early for the night. The neglected husband was lying next to his wife wearing his heavy silk embroidered dressing gown. His wife was stroking his chest and ruffling his dark wavy hair.

"Oh, you poor dear!" she said, "I shall have to see what I can do to prevent this calamitous decline."

Some while later, Sophy was on top of her husband, both drowsily satisfied.

"Am I too heavy?" she murmured, not really wanting to move as she lay on her husband's chest, breathing in the lovely smell of him, the combination of the bay rum soap he always used and his own indefinable scent.

"Never!" he replied, pulling her tighter. "I could lie like this forever."

"Me too, but I think I'm heavier now than before Sylvester. My bottom is bigger."

"Hm, let me see." Her husband lifted his shoulders and, uncovering her, looked down the length of her back to the hills of her buttocks. Then he lifted her off his chest and lay her on her stomach. He slid down the bed and inspected her derrière. "Your bottom looks perfect to me," he said, "and I'm recognized as something of a connoisseur."

As he moved back up next to her, Sophy remarked, "Virginie has a very round bottom." She was referring to the woman Lysander had been flirting with before he met her. After a failed attempt to win him back from Sophy, she had disappeared into the country. But now she was back, and cutting a swathe through the gentlemen of the *ton*.

"Does she? I can't remember," replied his lordship mendaciously. While he was the most uxorious of husbands and adored his wife, like all men, he could not avoid admiring a nice derrière or a generous bosom. These Virginie had, and to spare.

Sophy climbed back onto her husband till she lay nose to nose with him. "I don't believe you," she said and kissed him lightly on the lips. "But since you are feeling so neglected, I shall forgive you."

"It's true that neglect has affected my memory," mused his lordship. "I may need more looking after before it fully returns."

"If it is to help you remember Virginie Beaufort's bottom," retorted his wife, "I'm afraid my help with your loss of memory may not be as assiduous as you might want."

"Baggage!" chuckled her husband and gave her a loving tap on the part of the anatomy they had been discussing.

The following morning, which was peacefully Sylvester-free, the couple made another attempt to relieve his lordship's sense of neglect, and breakfasted in Sophy's bedchamber, as they had in the early days of their marriage. Then her ladyship went downstairs to see Mrs. Wilkins.

"Since Daisy is to be nursemaid, my lady," said the housekeeper, "she will need grey uniforms with white aprons, cuffs and caps. She cannot look after the young master dressed as a scullery maid. What I propose is that for the time being she borrow something from one of the upstairs maids. The seamstress will be here next week and I will have her make up two proper uniforms." She was referring to the itinerant needlewoman who visited the great homes on a rotating basis, staying as long as it took to do whatever sewing was needed.

"Better have her make three," responded her ladyship. "Daisy is bound to get dreadfully dirty dealing with Sylvester. And I'm not sure that white aprons are the best idea!"

"As you say, my lady," smiled the housekeeper. "The young master does seem to be able to find dirt no matter how hard one tries."

"But his father prefers that he be given opportunity to… er… explore the world. His lordship would rather he get dirty than be obliged to sit quietly. He tells me that he had a very controlled childhood himself and remembers often being unhappy."

The two women sat in silence for a moment, contemplating the sad idea of an unhappy child surrounded by everything money could buy, except what he wanted.

It was a fine spring morning and the rhododendrons were in bloom in the park, so after the interview with the housekeeper, Sophy and Lysander decided to take a ride there. Sophy loved riding in the curricle with her husband. She watched him as he deftly wheeled through the London traffic with mere inches to spare, without appearing to do more than give the most minor twitch to the reins. A wave of desire washed over her.

"I do love you," she murmured. Her lovely confection of a bonnet, with its blue feather just the color of her eyes, was turned up becomingly on the side closest to him, so she rubbed her cheek against his greatcoat. It is doubtful whether he heard her, with the din of the London streets, but at her touch he turned and gave her his charming smile. Her heart leaped.

They trotted in a leisurely fashion round the various paths of the park admiring the flowering shrubs. Sophy, an accomplished watercolorist, vowed to return and sketch the blooms one day soon.

Suddenly his lordship remarked, "I hope I may be mistaken, but I fear I see the future sixth Earl, quite covered in mud, playing with sticks in a puddle just over there."

He was not mistaken. Following his lordship's instructions, Daisy had taken Sylvester to the park that fine morning. After allowing him to run around for a while, she had taught him a puddle game she played with her brothers, in which each tried to sink the other's "boats" made of small sticks, with longer, narrower sticks. Sylvester found this game just to his taste but, needless to say, it was impossible to keep his boots, or the rest of him, from the muddy water.

When the curricle drew abreast of him, he was crying with delight, "I sinked your boats Daisy! I sinked them!"

Daisy was the first to notice the arrival of the Earl and his lady. She curtseyed in some confusion, "I'm sorry me lord, me lady. I didn't want 'im to get so muddy, but some'ow it just 'appened!"

Sylvester was looking at the fascinating puddle, where the sunken sticks had just popped up again. "Why they comed back?" he cried. "Yook, Daisy, they comed back!" Then he saw his parents. "Mama! Papa!" The boats were immediately forgotten. "I come up with you!" and he tried to clamber up the side of the vehicle.

"Just a minute, sir!" said his father sternly. "You are not coming anywhere near this curricle in those boots. Daisy, please remove them from his person and take them home for cleaning." Then, as she began to stammer apologies again, "No need to apologize. I should have warned you that muddy water is like a beacon to him. It's something of a family tradition. No damage is done, and Sylvester has learned a valuable lesson about flotation."

The young lord, boots removed, was delivered to his Papa's lap, where he was enveloped in his many-caped riding coat, with just his head showing above the buttons.

"I drive, Papa! I drive!" he said, trying to free his arms.

"Certainly not! I value my chestnuts too much. Stop wriggling or I shall take you to the carriage and you shall go home with Daisy. You shall not drive my horses but we'll be at Hale Court quite soon and you shall have a pony."

"A pony!" cried her ladyship. "Are you sure, Lysander? He's too young, surely!"

"I began riding at his age. Have no fear, he will be on a leading rein and Rogers will keep a sharp eye on him. The sooner he starts the better."

Her ladyship knew that the head groom was a careful man, but was not convinced. However, this was not the time for such a discussion. Sylvester, having heard the magic word 'pony' was quiet, contemplating that marvel for a while, but soon his thoughts reverted to the puddle.

"Papa!" he said suddenly in a puzzled tone, "I sinked Daisy's boats but they comed back. Why? I sinked them but they comed back."

"It's because wood floats, Sylvester. That means wood stays on top of the water. It wants to be on top, not underneath. When you push it under it goes down but it comes back up. It wants to float. That's why we make big boats out of wood. I'll take you to the river and you can see."

"I yike boats, Papa," said his son, "and I yike ponies," and, as an afterthought, "and I yike Daisy."

"So do I," agreed Papa.

When they arrived at Hale House, his lordship carried his son inside, still buttoned inside his coat. There they found the Honorable Charles Alverstoke waiting. He and Lysander had been fast friends since their Eton days and he was godfather to Sylvester.

"Nunckie Charles! Nunckie Charles!" cried the heir, and squirmed to be put down.

"Well, 'Vester," said Charles, squatting down to catch the child who was running to him as fast as his long little legs could carry him. "I say, where are your boots? Don't your Papa buy you any boots?"

"My boots is all muddy," said the child.

"Good God, not you, too?" replied Charles, picking up his godson. He was remembering the story of Lysander's first meeting with Sophy. What is it with you Hales and mud?"

"Don't bring all that up again, Charles," said Lord Hale, shaking his hand. "He was playing in the park."

"So you say," retorted Charles, and addressing his godson, "Look here, my man! Watch that muddy jacket on my new waistcoat. Mighty fine, ain't it?"

"It's fowers" responded Sylvester, looking at it. "My Mama yikes fowers."

"She's a fower herself," said Charles gallantly, going over to kiss Sophy on the cheek. Looking at her, then at her son, he said "Dammit, he looks more and more like you, Sophy, except for the Hale nose. Lucky feller! We all know what a good size hooter means."

"No," said Sophy, "What does it mean?"

But before anyone could enlighten her, Daisy came into the hall, curtseyed, and begged to take the young master down for his dinner.

"I've got 'is slippers, my lady, and I'll clean 'is boots directly."

"Daisy!" cried Sylvester, squirming to be put down. Charles obliged and he ran to his maid. "Daisy! Papa says sticks yike to be on top. They doesn't wants to go under!"

Daisy bobbed a curtsey and they left, Sylvester gabbling on about wood and floating and boats and ponies.

"That boy is as bad as his Papa," said Charles, shaking his head and following his friends into the family sitting room, "Prosin' on, prosin' on. Just keep him away from the Latin, that's all!"

Sophy laughed. She had heard numerous stories of how her husband had done more or less all of Charles' prep at Eton. Then, remembering, she asked, "What was all that about his nose?"

"Ah," said Charles, "well, it's just that…" and he looked towards Lysander in confusion.

"When will you learn to guard your tongue in mixed company, Charles?" chuckled his friend. "You spend too much time in sporting fraternities. What he means, my love, is that there is evidence, even in the classics I must say, that a man's nose is an indicator of the size of, let us say, his masculine equipment."

"Oh," said Sophy, then with dawning understanding, "Oh!" She blushed.

"Congratulations, Charles!" laughed his lordship. "You have made my wife blush, a thing I haven't been able to do in some time."

"I say, Sophy," said Charles, remorsefully, "I'm sorry, but, dammit, it's a good thing!"

"I suppose it is," smiled Sophy. "I have to admit, Charles, I learn some interesting things from you! And I do like your new waistcoat. It looks like spring."

Sophy always defended Charles' sartorial choices, though his waistcoats were an object of amusement to her husband, himself more soberly clad.

Pennyworth came in with a bottle of *Fino* and offered it to their guest and his lordship. He knew her ladyship rarely took alcohol and offered her instead a ratafia.

"You will stay for lunch, won't you, Charles?" invited Sophy.

"I was hoping you would say that," admitted Charles. "Fact is, I've got something I want to talk to you about, Sandy."

He was alone in using the nickname for his lordship, from the days they were at school together and he said *Lysander* was too much of a mouthful when he needed to yell for help.

"In that case, please tell Mrs. Green there will be one more for lunch, Pennyworth," said Sophy, intrigued, but too polite to ask what Charles might want to talk to her husband about.

"Oh, and Pennyworth, please tell Daisy that Sylvester may have a little of the trifle that is left, so long as he eats some vegetables with his dinner."

As her husband began to protest the profligate distribution of his trifle, Sophy laughed that he was as big a baby as Sylvester when it came to his favorite dessert. She said she was protecting them from the trifle-demanding invasion that would inevitably result if she did not allow their son to have some.

At lunch it did not take long for their garrulous guest to reveal the reason for his visit.

In answer to Sophy's "How are you going along, Charles?" he said, with a little hesitation, which was unlike him, "Fact is, I've popped the question to Georgianna and she said yes."

As his hosts expressed their pleased surprise, he continued, "Spoke to her father and he's happy with the union. M'father's still alive of course, but I'll be the Baronet one day. Point of fact, the Pater's not in prime twig. Thinking he might fall off the branch any day and I want to tie the knot before. Otherwise, might be months before we can do the deed. Can't get leg shackled during the period of mourning, and all that. Anyway, her Papa told me I had to see you, Sandy. Head of the family, y'know."

Georgianna was Lysander's youngest cousin, daughter of one of his two rather unpleasant aunts. Charles had met her on the occasion of the ball given by Lord Hale to introduce his wife to his family and the *ton*. She had been seventeen at the time, out for a year and a pretty girl practicing to be a shameless flirt. She and Charles had enjoyed each other's company, but no more than that. For the whole of the next season she had been a popular member of the younger set, from which the older Charles had been excluded. She had had a different beau every month. Then her exasperated family had sent her to the country for several months to help her older sister Mary, confined with her first child. From that she had returned a little less volatile, and the Hales had seen her in Charles' company quite often over the last year.

The idea that her beloved Charles with his carefree ways and startling waistcoats was to be married quite upset Sophy for a moment. He had been the first of Lysander's friends she had met. He had stood up for her husband at their wedding and then come to Hale Court to teach her to dance. He was himself a wonderful dancer. He was good humored and handsome in a muscular, stocky way. She could quite understand Georgianna falling in love with him. She was half in love with him herself.

He and Lysander were an odd couple. His lordship much taller and, though broad shouldered, of a slimmer build, and in character quite different. Charles was an avid sportsman, interested in all the races, boxing contests and ridiculous wagers that London had to offer. He would bet on just about anything. He read nothing but the sporting news and was a favorite in all the clubs, not least because he routinely but cheerfully lost at cards and was game for any wager, no matter how insane. He had recently won a quite fiercely bid bet as to the color of the hair of a newborn in one of the leading families. It was, as he had said, not an easy business handicapping the event, when no one was exactly sure who the father was.

Lysander was a good boxer and excellent fencer but preferred reading to watching sporting contests. Nowadays he rarely went to the clubs, where his dry humor might be missed but his ability to win at cards was not. Especially since the birth of his son, he preferred to be at home. Nevertheless, the two were firm friends and there was nothing one would not do for the other.

"Congratulations, Charles!" cried Sophy, putting her selfish thoughts out of her mind. "I hope you will be very happy. She is a lucky girl!" She left her chair to kiss his cheek.

"I will save my congratulations until we've had our talk, my friend," said her husband with mock seriousness. "After all, I may find some impediment that prevents you from being an appropriate choice for my cousin. I can already see one: your waistcoats cannot be considered suitable for the Great House of Hale."

"Oh, stow it, Sandy," said Charles, then stood and bowed to Sophy as she laughed and left them to it in the dining room.

CHAPTER FOUR

In which Lady Hale asks some questions

Although she was always glad to see Charles and particularly to hear his exciting news, Sophy was disappointed not to be able to be alone with her husband. She had been aroused ever since their curricle ride and had been looking forward to an afternoon dalliance. But since that was not possible, she went up to the nursery. There she found Sylvester taking his afternoon nap and Daisy in a chair by his bed, sewing buttons on her son's shirts. He was inclined to rip them off instead of undoing them, a chore he found annoying. "Just like his father," reflected her ladyship, thinking of the hooks that, on his instructions, her *modiste* had used instead of buttons on all her gowns. He too hated undoing buttons.

She asked if the young lord had eaten his vegetables.

"Oh yes, me lady," said Daisy, "I told him 'is Papa ate carrots, so 'e ate 'is, too. I read 'im a story before 'e went to sleep. I 'ope that's all right. I know the way I speak is not really proper, but I'm trying, me lady!"

"Thank you, Daisy. Don't worry about it on Sylvester's behalf. But for your own sake, I think it is a good idea. You will find that you are judged by the way you speak. It's not fair, but that's how it is. You may want one day to find employment as a nanny, and speaking the correct way will be absolutely necessary."

"Oh, me lady, I'll never leave 'Ale..." she corrected herself, "*H*ale *H*ouse. You are so good to me. Mrs. Simmons says I'm to 'ave *three* new dresses! Me mum will be so proud! And I loves the young master. 'E is such a funny little boy and ever so clever!"

There is no mother alive who does not like to hear that another thinks her child ever so clever, and her ladyship was no exception. She left the nursery thinking that her husband had shown great wisdom in the choice of a nursemaid.

Going downstairs, Sophy asked Pennyworth to call her carriage. The sun was quite warm and she decided to go outside and do some sketching. In the early days of their marriage, she and her husband had had a dreadful quarrel over her wanting to sketch unattended in the street. Her husband had ultimately given in, and now she went where she wanted, but never without telling either him or Pennyworth. When the weather was good, seated on her little stool with a shawl around her shoulders, since she found a pelisse or a cloak too confining, she had become a fairly common sight in the fashionable part of London. She was pointed out to newcomers as the lovely but eccentric Countess of Hale.

She had become quite a specialist in sketching aspects of the great homes she visited. In the winter she did indoor scenes: staircases, fireplaces, interesting doorways. In the better weather she liked to sketch the front doors. She turned all these into charming watercolors. The first ones she had done had been the magnificent carved fireplaces at Hale Court, each representing different local flora and fauna. Then she had done the Hale House front door in London, which bore a beautifully wrought knocker in the shape of a large script H, the Hale emblem which could be seen everywhere in both their homes.

Lysander laughed at this folly of the former Earls of Hale, but since it also appeared on the lining of his cloaks and greatcoats, and all the household linen, it was obvious he was proud of it. In fact, it had been the initial H that first alerted Sophy to who he was, since he had not introduced himself as Hale, but had used the family name, Barrington. She had teased him about it ever since, calling him "Mr. Barrington" whenever she thought he was getting above himself, and asking him if they should have an H embroidered on young Sylvester's nappies.

At one time, having seen the moody landscapes of Turner on show at the London home of the philanthropist John Julius Angerstein, Sophy had tried to copy his style, but she was forced to admit that her talent did not lie in that direction. Her works were pretty, that was all.

She always gave the finished watercolors to the family concerned, usually in thanks for an invitation to a ball or weekend visit. The hostesses who were lucky enough to have a "Lady Hale" hanging on their parlor walls considered themselves fortunate indeed.

In London, she had completed the front doors of the townhomes of the Keighly, Walsh, Flewett, Mayes, Davies, Burgess, Shepherd, Hargraves and Morrison families, and today she was going to sketch the Threlfall front door. Lady Threlfall was one of the leading socialites of London and entertained constantly. Sophy had noticed the lovely fanlight above the front door the first time she and her husband had been invited there. She told Pennyworth where she was going and left the house.

The gaslights were being lit in the streets when she finally made her way home. Lady Threlfall would not let her leave without inviting her in for tea, delighted that she was to be the latest recipient of a Lady Hale. She insisted that Sophy send away her carriage. The tea had led to a cozy gossip, but then Sophy had been forced to wait for the Threlfall barouche to bring her home. Now she was very late and she knew everyone would be wondering what had become of her. She came into the hall in a rush, scattering her sketchbook, pencils and stool and shawl. Footmen ran forward to pick it all up.

His lordship heard her precipitate arrival and came into the hall to see the footmen chasing rolling pencils and fluttering pages from her sketching pad. "I see you have returned, Lady Hale! And we wonder at our son's ability to sow ruin wherever he goes. Clearly he has it from his mother." He took her hands, saying "I'm glad you're home. I was beginning to get worried." Then, "Good God, your hands are frozen!"

"Lady Threlfall made me send home the carriage and have tea with her, then I had to wait for her barouche, and it made me much later than I intended. I am a little chilly, to tell the truth. I didn't have my cloak with me, only my shawl, and it grew quite cold after the sun went down. If I'd known I was going to be so late I'd have taken something heavier."

"That stupid woman! Why didn't she offer you a cloak?" said his lordship. "Pennyworth! Send Susan up for another shawl and bring her ladyship a brandy."

"Not brandy! I don't like it!" cried his wife.

"You shall have a sip," replied his lordship firmly, putting her shawl over her shoulders, bringing her to the fire and wrapping his arms around her.

When Pennyworth came in with the brandy and a second shawl, the Earl had his wife in a warm embrace. He coughed discretely, but neither of them paid any attention. He left the tray on a side table, the shawl beside it. A few moments later, when she was wrapped, protesting, in the second shawl and took her first sip of the brandy, Sophy made a face. But then she had to admit it did make her feel warmer. Her husband urged her to take another sip, but she refused any more.

"It's horrible!" she said.

"Good thing my father can't hear you. It's one of the great 1811 vintage that he laid down. You, my love, have no palate." His lordship drank the rest himself and led her out of the room.

Sylvester was bathed and in bed when his Mama and Papa arrived. He was chattering to Daisy about the boats he had seen that afternoon. After Charles had taken his leave, the fond Papa had taken his son to the docks to see the hundreds of ships there. It was said that by going from boat to boat, you could walk across the Thames down at the docks without getting your feet wet. Father and son had looked down into the murky water and seen how the boats floated, just like the sticks in the puddle.

"Those boats was 'normous," said Sylvester to Daisy and his mother. " And they was floating in the water. It was very dirty and smelly! Pooh! And you know what, Mama? We sawed a rat! But it ran 'way," he ended with disappointment.

When he said his prayers that night, as well as Mama and Papa and Daisy and Nunkie Charles, Sylvester prayed for the boats... and the rat.

Later that night, they had blown out the candles and were preparing to sleep when Sophy suddenly said, "Lysander, may I ask you something?"

"Of course. Anything!" he replied. "Is it an in-the-dark type of question? Are you blushing?"

"No! Well, maybe a little. It's about what Charles said about Sylvester's nose... and everything."

"Why do I think it's about the 'everything' that you want to talk, rather than the nose?" She could hear the smile in his voice.

"Well, the thing is... the thing is, how do I know?"

"How do you know what?"

"How do I know that your nose is an indication of the size of your... masculine equipment, as you put it? After all, I've never seen anyone else's, except those statues we saw in Italy and they were all much... smaller. I wondered about it at the time, but I was too shy to ask. *Is* yours particularly large? I mean, when I first saw it... you... I thought it looked huge, but I had nothing to compare it with."

"I'm glad I made such an impression!" laughed her husband. He was quiet for a moment. "I suppose I have to admit," he said finally, "it was quite a subject of discussion at Eton, but it's not something one usually talks about after one's school days. I believe it's something of a family trait, along with the nose. There have always been comments in the clubs about my grandfather and my father..." He did not finish the sentence, but continued, "On our wedding night, I was worried you might be afraid, but..."

"But I wasn't," finished Sophy. "How could I have been afraid? You were so gentle and thoughtful. Anyway," she added, "I liked it. I like it even more now." She mused, "I suppose it would be interesting to have a lover, though, then one could compare."

"He'd pay a high price just to be a source of comparison because I'd kill him."

She laughed. "Oh, Lysander! Lots of women have lovers. You know that because you were one of them. When you were younger."

"I'm deadly earnest," said his lordship. "I'd kill him."

"But no one killed you!"

"That's because I was discrete and the women were well known to be available. Their husbands were not likely to call one out."

"Everyone knew about Virginie Beaufort! Anyway, I would be very discrete, too."

"She wasn't married and discretion is not exactly her byword, as you know. As for you, discrete or not, I'd find out and I would call him out." He raised himself onto his elbow and looked at her in the dark. "I'm serious, Sophy!"

"Oh, don't be silly, Lysander!" said his wife. "You know I'm never going to do anything of the sort. I can't even bear the idea." She snuggled up to him.

"Good, neither can I. Is that the end of the questions?"

"Yes," said Sophy. Then, "No! Do you mean, you were so discrete, people won't remember who you had affairs with? If I asked, would people tell me?"

"Sophy!" said her husband, sitting up and speaking very seriously in the dark. "We are not continuing this discussion. You are not having any affairs, we both know you're not, and you are not going to try to find out about any of my previous... involvements. That is all over and done with. I've told you before, on my honor you are the only woman for me now, and you always will be. No more discussion." He lay back down.

They were both silent for a while. Then Lysander said, "I'm nervous when you're quiet. Just like Sylvester. When he's too quiet, he's up to no good. Come on, out with it!"

Sophy hesitated. "I do have another question. We talked about men, but now I wonder, are... are all women the same?" she said finally, "feel the same, I mean?"

"Good Lord, Sophy!" said her husband, sitting up again.

"It's not an unreasonable question, since we're on the subject. After all, how am I supposed to know if I don't ask, and you should know the answer!"

Lysander did not know what to say. After a moment of thought, he replied, "First of all, let me say that all women feel, as you put it, wonderful. Most men are usually so grateful a woman would let us... feel her, that we have no complaints. But no, the answer to your question is no, all women do not feel the same. But all feel very nice. Can we put that subject to rest now?"

"And me?" said Sophy, ignoring the last part of his response, "How do I feel, and do I feel different since I had Sylvester?"

"You, my love, feel perfect," he replied, rolling above her in the dark and supporting himself on his elbows. "And no, no difference since the birth of our son, although how that can be is a mystery beyond all mysteries." He kissed her lightly.

"Thank you. You are perfect too. I'm sure all your other lady friends thought so as well."

"Sophy!" said his lordship, warningly.

His wife kissed him lovingly and said no more, but all the same, she could not help wondering.

CHAPTER FIVE

In which Sophy does a little research

Over the next week, Sophy finished the watercolor of the Threlfall front door. It looked very pretty, with the fanlight reflecting the blue sky and scattered clouds of the fine spring day when she had done the sketch. She signed it with her now customary SLR. Originally, she had either not signed her pieces, or signed them SB, since Barrington was her married name. But she realized the hostesses to whom she gave the little gifts actually took pleasure in their being recognized as the work of Lady Hale, so she had taken to signing them SLH.

She knew that Lady Threlfall liked to gossip and it was with some deliberation, therefore, that she sent that lady a note, asking her if she would be at home at teatime two days hence. The response came, as she had expected it would, that her ladyship would be delighted to receive Lady Hale at four o'clock the following Friday.

His lordship was in the ballroom with Sylvester on his lap playing the piano when she left. The whole house rang with the discordant notes of her son's enthusiastic banging on the keys. In vain did Lysander attempt to show him the first four notes of *Baa Baa Black Sheep,* singing along with the notes. He might just manage to hit the correct key twice for the *Baa Baa*, but it degenerated into a wild racket after that.

"Sylvester, my son, you have a tin ear," announced his father. "Go and play with a drum in the nursery. You may as well bang on that instead of ruining the piano. You've already made enough of a mark on the rest of the room."

The Erard pianoforte in the ballroom had been purchased in Paris by his lordship's grandmother, who had admired the *rocaille* French style. It was she who had decorated Hale House in the style of Louis XV, with painted ceilings and curved-back gilded armchairs and settees upholstered in gold and ivory silk. Sophy had repainted the tops of the fine-legged side tables in the ballroom, stained over the years by wet glasses. She had also had glass tops cut to fit them, hoping to save them from further damage.

It certainly protected them from the many guests at the balls the Hales held every year, but it was not proving to be enough to protect them from the future sixth Earl. He had discovered the ballroom when his father introduced him to the piano for the first time, but it was not the piano that interested him. The gold spindle-back chairs lined up for guests needing a respite from dancing stretched from one end of the room to the other. Sylvester liked to try to leap from one to the other all the way down, or slide down the length of the parquet dance floor on his stomach. As a result, some of the little tables had crashed over, resulting in broken glass and splintered legs.

Dismissing his son, his lordship turned back to the keys and began to improvise on *Baa Baa Black Sheep, Hickory Dickory Dock,* and *Lavender Blue Dilly Dilly.* Daisy, who was sitting in one of the gold chairs staring wonderingly at the ceiling, which showed nymphs and shepherds dancing in bucolic scenes, turned her attention to his lordship, whose long fingers flew over the keys apparently without effort.

"Listen to your Papa, Sylvester," she said. "Listen to the lovely music!"

But her young charge had heard the word *drum* and was already pulling her out of the ballroom and towards the nursery.

"Don't let him bully you, Daisy," warned his lordship. "Remember you are the adult!"

"'Ave no fear, me lord," replied the nursemaid firmly. "'E will mind me!"

Sophy had meanwhile taken the carriage to the Threlfall mansion, where she was warmly greeted by the lady of the house. Once in the salon, she had handed over the watercolor of the front door to great acclaim. It was so pretty! It was exactly like! Lord Threlfall would be delighted! How clever she was!

Once this effusion had passed and tea had been served, Sophy turned the conversation by degrees to the subject she wanted to discuss. Luckily, her hostess loved nothing so much as a good gossip.

"I understand, Lady Threlfall, that you have been in London during the season for several years. I'm a relative newcomer myself, as you know," she began.

"Please call me Clara and I shall call you Sophy. I'm sure we are to be good friends! Yes, I have been here every season since my own coming out. That was, oh, five or six years ago." Lady Threlfall shaved five years off her age without a blink.

"My goodness, Clara! I never would have thought you were a year over twenty-five. You must have come out when you were fourteen!"

Lady Threlfall beamed. "You are too kind. But yes, my dear, I am quite the old… quite the *habituée* of London Society."

"Then I imagine you must have known my husband when he was younger. I'm told he was quite popular with the ladies. I wish I'd known him then! It's hard to imagine now that he's a devoted Papa."

"Oh yes, my dear! He had a new flirt every month! He was so charming, you see. We were all in love with him, even I! That was before I had an understanding with Lord Threlfall, of course."

"But I've been told he never had more than just a mild flirt with unmarried girls. His more serious… involvements were with married women or widows. They are no doubt older than you (an untruth, since she guessed Clara was of the same age as Lysander's likely conquests), but I don't suppose you knew any of them?"

Lady Threlfall threw up her hands, "Oh, my dear, please excuse me, for anyone can see that his lordship is absolutely devoted to you now, but there were so many over the years! Let me see… Lizzy Ponsonby, one remembers of course, because her husband sent her to their place in the country in the end, after she caused such a scandal, not with Lysander, of course, but with Henry Guilfoyle. Then there was… let me see, Nell Greenwood, Polly Oldkirk… Prissy Westover, Maria Cholmeley." She pondered for a moment, "Oh, yes, I remember! Pippa

Acton, Alice Farley... and that dark-haired woman... now, what was her name?... Goodness! I've forgotten! And of course, Virginie Beaufort, just before you were married. Off the top of my head that's who I remember."

Her hostess was quiet for a moment, reflecting. "The only unexpected one was Sally Joliffe, if what one heard was true, though it may just have been an *on-dit*. If it was so, Hale was her only indiscretion. She's a dear creature, Bunny Joliffe's wife. Used to be very pretty. Let herself go a bit now. Of course, Bunny hasn't been exactly the ideal husband. Other women, you know. Such a shame. There was talk that she and Lysander... but Hale was, well, still is, devastatingly attractive. You know that, of course! Tell me, my dear, is it true he found you somewhere in a ditch in the country?"

This was a story that had circulated in the clubs when Sophy and Lysander were first married. It had infuriated his lordship.

Sophy gave a little laugh, "Oh that old rumor! Of course not. But think how romantic! Goodness! Is that five o'clock I hear striking? I had completely lost track of time. My dear Lady... Clara, I must run. My husband is expecting me. We are to the opera this evening. I hope we will see you there? What a delightful cose we've had!"

With expressions of mutual esteem, they parted.

Early in her marriage Sophy had learned that one went to the opera as much or perhaps more, to be seen as to see the production. She therefore put on the latest creation made for her by Marianne, the most expensive *modiste* in London. This lady had for many years been a high priced *fille de joie* introduced to Lysander by his father. She had always wanted to open a superior dress-making establishment, and when he became the fifth Earl, Lysander had financed her.

Unlike the slim, straight empire style gowns that had been in style when she married, the fashion now was for dresses with somewhat fuller skirts, the bodice shaped down to just above the waist. This ideally suited Sophy with her slim body and full bosom, though she sometimes wondered if she should start wearing a corset, as many women did. Her husband frowned mightily at this suggestion, saying it was a damned difficult item for him to remove and vetoed it absolutely.

Her ladyship's gown for the opera was of a midnight blue taffeta that reflected the lovely color of her eyes. It had a low décolletage from which her white shoulders rose in all their glory. It was completed with short puffed sleeves and a wide embroidered silver band around the lower skirt, together with a matching silver shawl. It rustled beautifully when she walked, much to the delight of young Sylvester who said it sounded like his friend the mouse. He attempted to duck under her skirts to find the mouse, but was reprimanded by his father.

"Sylvester!" he said severely, "it is true that we men always wish to investigate beneath a lady's skirts, but it is an urge a gentleman must control." He took Sophy's hand and kissed her palm. "You look wonderful, my love. Your gown is most becoming and Susan has arranged your hair to perfection. I am a lucky man." He kissed her lightly on the lips.

Sophy was wearing her sapphire and diamond parure. These had been gifts from Lysander early in their marriage. The necklace and earrings sparkled around her neck and Susan had fixed the detachable pendant in her hair. Sophy's natural curls fell in ringlets at the back from the top knot. The matching bracelet had been placed on top of her elbow-length blue silk gloves. No one would recognize the impoverished countrywoman the Earl had met by accident. She smiled at her husband, suffering a momentary pang that she had deliberately gone against his wishes in asking questions about the paramours in his earlier life. But, she reasoned, everyone else in London society knew about it all, why should not she?

They were to meet Charles Alverstoke and his intended at the Theatre Royal in Covent Garden where the House of Hale held a box. That evening they were to see a comic opera called *Clari the Maid of Milan*. It was frankly not very engaging except for one song, *Home Sweet Home,* which the audience appreciated, to judge from the number of curtain calls.

During the intermission, while the Earl was talking to one of the many people who stopped by their box, Sophy complimented Charles on his latest waistcoat, a green satin affair with vertical black stripes, which actually was quite difficult to look at for very long. Then she asked if he knew a gentleman called Bunny Joliffe.

"Good Lord, Sophy," said Charles in his irrepressible way, "what do you want to know about that old dog?"

"Oh, nothing really," she said carelessly. "It's just a name that came up and... and I thought it was odd for a man to be called Bunny. I understand his wife is Sally. It sounds like something from a children's story: Bunny and Sally," she improvised. "Are they here?"

"Suppose it does, now that you mention it! Yes. That's old Bunny over there."

He pointed to a late middle-aged man with a full head of grey hair and heavy side whiskers. It was clear he had once been handsome, but now he was corpulent and his face bore the broken veins of a heavy drinker. He was laughing loudly at something one of his companions was saying.

"And Sally?" prompted Sophy.

"Sally? She's over there on the end of that row." Charles indicated a woman who Sophy guessed was in her thirties but looked older. She wore a lace cap over a coiffure of faded blond curls and was obviously strictly corseted in a red and yellow check gown. She had a very pretty face which was marred by a look of anxiety, especially as she looked towards her husband. At that moment she looked in Sophy's direction, and Sophy nodded and smiled. The smile was returned, though not without some puzzlement.

"She must have been lovely when she was younger," remarked Sophy.

"Yes, a real corker. Sandy used to…" He stopped in some confusion.

"Sandy used to what?"

Charles hesitated. "Er… he used to like her," he ended lamely.

"Was she married then?"

"Y...es. But you know... Bunny... Bunny had an eye for the girls. Always has. Look here, Sophy, why all these questions?"

"Oh, I don't know. No reason. It's just interesting. You've been in and out of London all your life. You know everybody's history. I don't."

The bell sounded for the beginning of the second half of the opera and their conversation ended, much to Charles' relief.

At the supper bespoke by his lordship after the opera, there were outraged cries as he begged Charles to remove his waistcoat. He said it was it was putting him off his supper. Charles responded by caroling the chorus of *Hoome Sweeet Hoome* in his tuneless bellow. Then Sophy and Georgianna were able to chat about the upcoming wedding. Sophy was amazed to hear Charles spoken of as the Great Arranger. Charles had arranged for them to be married at St. George's Church, Hanover Square at the end of May, said Georgianna. Charles said they would not have to go straight into the family home if she did not care to live with his mother. Charles said they could live in a rented house until he came into his inheritance. Charles said he would persuade his Mama to remove to the Dower house when the time came. Charles would be able to arrange it all. Sophy was secretly very doubtful. Charles with his devil-may-care attitude? It was hard to imagine him as the head of the family. She felt sure he was more likely to go to a horse race than look at house leases. But she nodded her agreement and said nothing.

"What were you and Charles in deep conversation about at the opera?" asked his lordship on the way home in the carriage.

"Oh, the wedding, you know," dissembled Sophy, with another pang, and subtly shifted the conversation. "By the way, I told Georgianna you would pay for her wedding clothes. I shall take her to Marianne next week. You did that for Mary, you remember, so I thought you would not object." Georgianna's elder sister had met her future husband at Sophy's coming-out ball, too. Both she and her husband had a very soft spot for Mary.

When her husband merely gave a slight shrug of acquiescence, she continued, "Georgianna seems convinced that Charles will arrange everything: the wedding, where they will live, persuading his mother to move when the time comes. Everything. Do you think that he will in fact be able to manage the family? He seems so unsuited."

"Oh, he'll rise to it," responded her husband. "I know he seems to care for nothing but fun, but he can be much more level-headed than you think."

Sophy and Lysander had gone through a bad patch four years ago because Sophy, unfamiliar with the unwritten rules of the *ton*, had refused to listen to her husband. As a result, her name had been bandied about in the clubs. It was Charles who had smoothed it over and prevented Lysander taking violent action, but Sophy knew nothing of that.

"I hope so. Georgianna is only two years younger than me, but she seems so child-like. She is absolutely depending on Charles."

"The way you depend on me, my love?" teased his lordship. 'I know you look to me constantly for direction!"

"Don't tease, Lysander! I know I like to do things my own way, but I do depend on you. Our whole life runs smoothly because of you. I never have to worry; I just know everything will be as it should." She moved close to him and leaned her head against his shoulder.

"Not if Master Sylvester has his way," laughed her husband, kissing the top of her head. "Nothing will be as it should! He seems intent on destroying the house. Good thing we're going to the country soon, I just hope we can survive till then!"

CHAPTER SIX

In which her ladyship makes an acquaintance

"He looks so sweet when he's sleeping!" whispered Sophy to her husband when, on their return from the opera, they went to the nursery to see their son.

"He looks just like you, with his curls all over the pillow," responded her husband, taking her in his arms. "Which is how I want to see you in about ten minutes. You ignored me all evening, spending your time in conversation with Charles."

"Oh, is it a conversation you'll be wanting?" Sophy looked at him under her lashes.

"Baggage!" replied her husband, and smacked her lightly on the bottom.

It was rather more than ten minutes before Sophy dismissed Susan. Her maid was almost unrecognizable from when she had first become a lady's maid. She was from a large family and her father was one of the Hale estate tenants. She had originally been engaged as a house maid, but had proved so adept at dealing with Sophy's unruly curls that she had become her personal maid. While still a small, slim person, with the good diet and happy working conditions, she had filled out and become quite pretty. She wore the plain, high-throated, lace-collared dress of her status, but since her ladyship made sure she was kept up to date with the fashion, it was well cut; it fitted into her narrow waist and the fuller skirt enhanced her shape. Sophy had given her a cameo as a Christmas gift two years before, and she wore it nearly every day in the center of her lace collar. She looked every inch a lady's maid, and was afforded the appropriate status amongst the downstairs staff. At the servants' dining table, she sat next opposite Winton, his lordship's valet, only one place below the butler and the housekeeper.

Lysander came into his wife's room as Susan left. He was wearing the heavy silk dressing gown he had owned ever since his wife had known him. Sophy had always loved the sight of her husband in it. It reminded her of their wedding night, and on the rare occasions he was away, she would take it to her bed and bury her face in it, loving its Lysander smell.

Sophy's bedchamber was in the same style as the public rooms downstairs. The ceiling was painted with barely-veiled maidens and their swains cavorting in leafy bowers, and the bed and matching dressing table were decorated with festoons of roses held aloft by rosy-bottomed cherubs. The bed curtains, draperies and soft furnishings were all pink and ivory, and the Aubusson rug had a border of roses. Sophy loved it all, but in spite of frequent repairs, the bed was again creaking ominously. His lordship kept threatening to replace it. Tonight he regarded it with a jaundiced eye.

"I'm not getting into that bed again," he announced. "I know it will one day deposit both of us on the floor and splinters will lodge in my back and your bottom. My back I don't care about, but your bottom is a matter of great concern to me."

Sophy laughed but followed him back into his room, from which the *rocaille* furnishings had been erased and only the white and gilt painted walls hinted of how it had been in his grandfather's time. Upon coming into the Earldom, Lysander had replaced all the furniture with the solid mahogany and rosewood furniture of the French Empire. There were large gold animal paws at the ends of the legs of the gleaming console table and his desk had a wide dark surface scattered with open books and newspapers. The high bed was a massive affair with a rolled back headboard.

"I was never a supporter of that devil Bonaparte," said Lysander after a while, "but I'm damned glad he made the fashion for this style of bed. I can only suppose he and Josephine had the same trouble you and I do in the rose bower. She was quite a buxom wench by all accounts, and," he added, with a sidelong look at his wife, "she was nicely rounded, I'm told."

Sophy laughed, but it gave her a pang, thinking of Sally Joliffe who had probably been like Josephine in that respect, and it was a while before she slept.

The next morning, his lordship took himself off to Gentleman Jackson's boxing salon, where he went at least twice a week. He was, as Charles had once told her, "handy with his bunches of fives" and enjoyed the exercise. Sophy took Daisy and Sylvester to the park in her carriage. Her husband had purchased this smart equipage about a year earlier to replace the one he had given her in the first months of their marriage. She had protested that there was nothing wrong with the old one, but his lordship had insisted she be seen in nothing that was not the *dernier cri*.

When they were first married, Sophy, who was brought up almost penniless, had not wanted to spend more than her quarterly allowance, and since she bought gifts or gave a good deal of it away, she had appeared many times in the same gowns. The mean-spirited jokes in his clubs about his apparently keeping her short of money were one of the things that had caused trouble between them early on. Ever since then, Lysander had insisted on her appearing as expensively turned out as possible.

On this occasion he had bought her a cabriolet with a large retractable hood that could be drawn over in bad weather. It was painted a glossy black with a blue leather interior and white trim, which his lordship chose, he said, because blue always made him think of her. It bore the gold script H and Hale crest on the sides. He teasingly told her he had decided on this identification because he wanted other drivers to recognize the carriage and give her a wide berth. In fact, there was truth in what he said. Sophy could drive herself, but she was not a courageous whipster and felt very insecure in London traffic when other carriages came so close. She usually only went as far as the park. Two liveried grooms stood up behind and one would jump down to take the reins if necessary.

At the park, Sophy tried to interest Sylvester in drawing one of the many blossoms that were so lovely in the spring. But he was having none of it.

"You draw fowers, Mama," he pronounced finally. "I play ball with Daisy."

Daisy was now wearing the appropriate uniform for a nursemaid. Her long-sleeved grey gown, cut high to the neck, had plain white removable collar and cuffs, and was covered by a long white apron. The style suited her spare frame. Her hair, which was quite thick and wavy, was parted in the center, and drawn into a knot at the back of her neck. She wore a grey wool cloak and a simple black bonnet. The whole ensemble gave her dignity and made her look somewhat older, which she considered a good thing. She could not wait for her family to see her, and was looking forward to the Hales' removal to Hale Court, close to them, in the early summer.

Charles had given his godson a ball made from a pig's bladder covered in leather. It was an expensive toy, and Daisy thought how her brothers would love it. She used to play with them using an old bottle tied around with many layers of rags. They would try to kick it between two sticks, while their opponents tried to stop them, frequently leading to bruised shins, either from the flying bottle or from a mis-aimed boot. She was mindful of this as she stood between two sticks stuck in the grass and fielded her young charge's enthusiastic but often misdirected kicks. She hit upon the ruse of letting him kick the ball between the two sticks without intercepting it, but then having him begin again from some distance away. This had the double advantage of having her receive fewer blows to the shins and tiring out his young lordship. Sophy, observing this, thought again how right her husband had been in offering Daisy this job.

Sophy had been dividing her time between sketching and watching her son and was a little surprised to hear a low, musical voice say, "Lady Hale, I believe?"

She turned to see Sally Joliffe addressing her from a carriage. Next to her sat a girl of perhaps fifteen years, a pretty blond young woman, obviously her daughter.

"I am Sally Joliffe. Forgive me for interrupting you. We are not acquainted, but I saw you yesterday evening at the opera and you nodded so kindly. This is my daughter Ruth."

"Oh," said Sophy, rising from her stool. "Yes, Mrs. Joliffe. I am so pleased to meet you, and your daughter." She bowed slightly towards Ruth, who did the same. "I was taking tea with Lady Threlfall yesterday and she mentioned your name. It was such a coincidence that I happened to see you at the opera."

"I had heard that you were a gifted artist," pursued Sally Joliffe, "and now I see it's true. You have captured that rhododendron perfectly."

"Do you think so?" replied Sophy, wrinkling her nose. "I'm not sure. But it will look better when I have painted it, I think. Watercolor covers a multitude of sins!" she laughed.

"Oh, Mama," cried Ruth, "look at that little boy over there. He just slid quite three feet in the grass and the back of his coat is covered in green! I wonder his nursemaid permits it!"

"I'm sorry to say, that is my son, Sylvester," laughed Sophy. "He has a positive genius for making himself dirty, no matter how one may try. It's not Daisy's fault." And raising her voice, she cried, "Sylvester! Please come here and make your bow to Mrs. Joliffe and Ruth."

The young lord showed some reluctance to leave his game until Daisy took his hand and led him to where his mother was standing. She bobbed a curtsey and whispered to her charge, "Go on, Sylvester. Make your bow just like your Papa has taught you."

Thus encouraged, he bowed stiffly to each of the ladies and said "'Vester Barrington, Ma'am, 'tyour service."

Then he lifted his blue eyes to his mother and said, "I go an' play with the ball now?" Upon receiving an affirmative nod, he smiled radiantly and ran off, with Daisy in his wake.

"What a sweet little boy!" said Ruth at the same time as her mother murmured, "His smile is just like his father's," and then looked down at her gloved hands in some confusion.

"Yes," replied Sophy quickly, in an attempt to cover Sally Joliffe's obvious embarrassment, "he is a sweet little boy most of the time, but he has so much energy! He never means to, but he creates havoc in the home!"

"I only have daughters," said Sally Joliffe, recovering. "They're perhaps easier to raise in the beginning, but harder later on." She was thinking of the costs and difficulty of bringing out two daughters in three years. Ruth, at fifteen, had a younger sister who was twelve, and a great deal of expense was therefore inevitable quite soon, a necessity for which her husband frequently voiced his displeasure.

"That may be so," replied Sophy with a smile, "but I have quite enough on my hands at the moment, and it's hard to look ahead!"

The driver muttered that the horses should not stand any longer, and the Joliffe ladies took their leave, with kind expressions on all sides.

Sophy was convinced by Sally Joliffe's embarrassed comments that she had been one of her husband's liaisons. She considered how, or indeed if, she should further the acquaintance. She caught sight of her groom as he walked the horses nearby, and signaled for him to come to pick them up. It was time for Sylvester's dinner and her lunch. Should she tell her husband about meeting Sally Joliffe, she wondered? Probably not.

Just as Sophy, Sylvester and Daisy were descending from her carriage in front of Hale House, his lordship drew up in his new high perch phaeton, a vehicle he had taken to driving when he was alone. Sophy found it alarming and rarely went in it. With its enormously high wheels, the driver's seat was nearly eight feet off the ground, and even with a step to help, mounting and dismounting was not easy. Sylvester immediately cried, "Up, Papa, up!" and tried to climb up the side of the carriage.

"Steady on, sir!" called his lordship from his high perch. "Stop scratching the paintwork."

At a nod from him, his tiger Jeb, who rode at the back of the phaeton, jumped down and handed Sylvester up to his Papa's lap. The child squealed in delight and cried, "Go,

Papa! Go!" The fond father allowed his horses to walk forward a few paces, but reined them in almost immediately. In spite of angry protests from his son, his lordship then handed him back down to his tiger and then jumped down himself.

"Don't take on so, young master!" admonished Jeb. "You take a tumble from up there and it will be bellows to mend with you."

As his son continued to complain vociferously, his Papa intervened. "Sylvester, that's enough!" he said in a tone his son recognized as final. "Go inside immediately. You will not make this fuss on the doorstep. You are Sylvester Barrington, not a circus performer. Act appropriately!"

Chastened, his son went indoors, where, seeing Daisy with his ball, he immediately cheered up.

Meanwhile, the Earl had taken his wife's elbow and ushered her into the hall. He turned to her with a smile. "In that delicious bonnet, I should not allow you to be seen in public without me," he said, "You are so pretty I fear you will be stolen away!" He bent and kissed her on the cheek.

Sophy, feeling guilty about her encounter with Sally Joliffe, did not know how to respond. Just then, eager to be back in his father's good graces, Sylvester ran up to his Papa saying,

" 'N the park, Papa, I made my bow to a lady. She had a funny name. Jolly! Mrs. Jolly! In't that funny, Papa?"

"Joliffe," said Sophy quickly. "It was Mrs. Joliffe and her daughter."

"Sally Joliffe?" His lordship looked at her hard and raised an enquiring eyebrow. "I didn't know you were acquainted with her."

"I'm not... really. She stopped to look at my sketch of the rhododendrons, that's all. Her daughter Ruth was with her. They are very like."

His lordship looked at her quizzically, but said nothing. They went into lunch.

CHAPTER SEVEN

In which her ladyship gives advice

The following week, Sophy arranged to take Georgianna to the *modiste,* to be fitted for wedding clothes. Before they left, the married lady took the maiden into her bedchamber for a sensitive conversation.

"Georgianna, my dear," she began, feeling like her grandmother, though there were only two years between them, "forgive me for my indelicacy, but I wonder how much you know about the... the act between husband and wife." She smiled inwardly as she remembered the very similar way the vicar's wife, her friend at home, had begun the same topic. That good woman, Mrs. Bradshaw, had told her that she must always comply with her husband's wishes in the bedroom. Though it was a messy affair, she said, her husband, a gentleman, would manage it all. There might even be some pleasure in it later. For Sophy, it had been an experience which she had enjoyed from the start and indeed now longed for, but Georgianna might be made of different stuff.

It became clear that Georgianna knew nothing at all. Sophy, who had been born and raised in the country, had at least been aware of the nature of the physical act, but her younger friend was ignorant. Her mother had been even less forthcoming than Mrs. Bradshaw, contenting herself with saying merely that her daughter should obey her husband. Though reassuring, since she could not imagine her darling Charles asking her to do anything she did not like, this left Georgianna none the wiser. She had some idea that kissing was all that was required, though she said blushingly she did think her husband would want to see her body. Sophy explained to her as delicately as she could what would actually happen, and, indeed, what real kissing was, leaving Georgianna red-faced and round-eyed.

"Look," said Sophy finally. "I will have Marianne, Madame Deville, explain it to you more fully. She is much more... experienced than I and will be able to give you... hints. She helped me once."

When Sophy had sought Marianne's advice in the early days of her marriage, the *modiste*'s words had been matter-of-fact and not embarrassing, so she felt her the best person for Georgianna to consult. She did not think Charles would be unkind, but neither did she think he was especially articulate, and Georgianna seemed so innocent. Besides, Sophy felt strongly that the more women knew about their own bodies, the better. Sophy had promised Lysander never to reveal Marianne's previous occupation. But luckily, Georgianna did not appear to find it strange that the *modiste* should be able to give this type of advice.

On Sophy's assertion that Marianne had perfect taste, Georgianna was happy to be led by her. Seeing the bride's sweet fair prettiness, the *modiste* thought a very pale pink gown might best become her. From a recent *Mode Illustrée* from Paris, they chose a chastely scooped-neck gown with a palest of pink taffeta underdress, quite slim, and a sheer overdress featuring a wide ruched band of darker pink around the hem, under the bosom and around the edge of the elbow-length sleeves. It would have only a demi-train as Madam thought Georgianna not tall enough for a long one. The veil would be of the same sheer materials as the overdress. It would be both youthful and elegant. Since the couple would be going to Italy after the wedding, the women also chose a travelling gown and two light summer dresses suitable for the Italian weather.

"I didn't ask you before, but you will be my bridesmaid, won't you, Sophy?" asked Georgianna anxiously. "I would feel so much more comfortable with you there! I did ask my sister Mary, but she is increasing again, you know. I would love her little girl to scatter rose petals in front too, so... please don't think me forward, Sophy, but do you think I could have some roses from the Court?" Hale Court had a profusion of roses, planted by Lysander's great-great-grandmother and carefully tended by the head gardener.

"I would be very pleased to be your bridesmaid, though I'm not exactly a maid! How delightful! I'll have Madame make me a gown in the darker pink of yours. It's not a color I usually wear, so it will be something new. And don't worry about the roses. I'm sure I can ask for some from the masses they have at the Court. You remember them at my first ball? But don't they make your Mama sneeze and that's why she never visits us there?"

"Oh, Mama! She pretends to sneeze because she was jealous of Lysander's mother. She was so pretty, you see, and she was the Countess. My mother and Aunt Dorothea were never exactly beautiful, as you know. Aunt Dorothea has the Hale nose. It looks good on Lysander, but... well. Anyway, they never go to Hale Court."

"Well, I hope you and Charles will come often. We are there usually there from June till the end of October, after the harvest. Anyway, I'm going to leave you with Madame now, while I look at patterns for my new gown. Don't be shy to ask her anything!"

Sophy spent a delightful hour perusing the newest pattern books and looking at fabrics. She did not want to compete with the bride, and chose a simple model with short puffed sleeves and a boat neckline. The skirt fell in an inverted V shape from just above the waist. The underdress would be in the darker pink silk from Georgianna's dress, and the silk overdress could be embroidered with the same color. The pattern called for ruffles over the bosom, but Sophy thought she would dispense with those, not wanting to draw any more attention to that part of her anatomy. As a married lady, she would wear a lace cap, of course; as a bridesmaid she could hardly wear a bonnet. She smiled ruefully at the idea and wondered what Lysander would say. When Georgianna and Marianne emerged from their cose, she showed the pattern and fabrics to the *modiste*. The latter was a little doubtful about making anything in pink for her ladyship, and suggested that the overdress would be best in a delicate ivory lace. The pink would show through but be diffused. This being agreed, and with the understanding that the no doubt staggeringly high bills would be sent to his lordship, they parted with expressions of thanks.

In the carriage, Georgianna was full of praise for Madame. "She was so direct, yet not embarrassingly so," she said. "Thank you for having me speak with her. I was woefully ignorant, I realize that now. I shall be much calmer on my wedding night... I think. Oh, Sophy, is it so very dreadful? It sounds awful!"

Sophy patted her hand. "No, it's not dreadful at all. In fact, it's nice... very nice... when you get used to it. It hurts a bit the first time, I'm sure Marianne told you that, but only for a moment. I suppose it depends on... on the size of... of everything, but I can tell you that even though Lysander is quite... well, let me say it straight... quite large, it was not awful at all. It was wonderful, actually."

She thought for a moment about her own wedding night and smiled inwardly. "I think you should ask Mary if she used something to... to make it easier. A balm or something you can use. I'm sure you understand. And about babies. She must do... something."

Sophy herself had been helped by a balm made by Lysander's old Nanny but she felt Georgianna's sister would be a more appropriate resource for her young friend.

She drove the younger woman home, and could not escape without going in to greet her husband's aunt. This was never a very pleasant duty, since that lady seemed to find fault wherever she could.

"I suppose you've spent a great deal of money," she said to the young women, without an iota of gratitude in her tone. "Lucky for you that Lysander can afford it, I'm sure. I don't know what I am to wear. I shall get out the gown I wore for Mary's wedding, I suppose. It's only three years old."

"Dear Aunt Mildred," replied Sophy, fighting back a stinging retort, for she knew his lordship provided amply for both his aunts, and their husbands had money of their own, "I'm sure Lysander would be happy to pay for your gown, too. Please have a new one made and send him the bill. I will tell him I said you could do so."

"I suppose I can't go to Madame Deville…"

"Oh, no!" said Sophy quickly, not wanting to expose Marianne to this nip-cheese of a customer who she would never be able to get rid of and who would never be happy, "I'm afraid she will be much too busy the next month. She is making four gowns for Georgianna and one for me, apart from her other clients. But your regular dressmaker will be pleased to do it, I'm sure."

"*Four* gowns! Good gracious, Georgianna," cried her mother, "you are fortunate indeed to enjoy the favor of your cousin! *Four* gowns! and from Madame Deville's! Wait till I tell Dorothea!" Lysander's aunt, knowing that Madame Deville was quite the most expensive *modiste* in London, and enjoying the prospect of putting her elder sister's nose out of joint, was momentarily mollified.

Luckily, at that moment, her husband came into the room. Sophy liked him very much. He was a quiet, unassuming man with a wry sense of humor. Lysander and she had often wondered why he had chosen such a harridan as Mildred as his wife. "She probably chose *him* because she could bully him, and he was too afraid to put up a fight," was her husband's assessment. But Sophy had always considered that there was more steel in him than was immediately apparent.

He greeted Sophy with a bow, and kissed her hand. "Well, hussy!" he said turning to his daughter with a smile and kissing her on the cheek, "have you enjoyed your gallivanting and spending other people's money?"

"Oh, yes, Papa," replied Georgianna. "Just think! Besides the most beautiful wedding dress, I am to have a travelling gown and *two* summer dresses for Italy! And Sophy says cousin Lysander will pay for Mama's dress too, only Madame Deville won't be able to make it."

"That is more than generous," said her Papa, "but we can pay for your Mama's gown ourselves." He turned to his wife, "I know you will not want to place that added burden on Hale. He is offering us the wedding breakfast, as you know, since you claimed we have not the space here. That is above enough."

As his wife began to splutter, he said to Sophy with a bow, "Thank you, my dear, and please convey our sincere thanks to his lordship."

Sophy reported this to her husband later that night when they had retired to bed. He laughed and said, "I'll wager Mildred was mad as a hornet after you left. I'm glad I wasn't in his shoes."

"I think he's made of sterner stuff than you think. Perhaps he secretly keeps her on a short lead, and that's why she's always so unpleasant. Anyway, I like him, and I like Georgianna. I think she will make Charles a good wife. She obviously loves him and wants to make him happy."

She had no intention of telling Lysander that she had asked Marianne to talk to his young cousin about the private side of married life. For some reason, she felt he would not approve.

However, she did say, "But do you know, Lysander, she wa... is completely ignorant about the... physical side of marriage. She thou... thinks that all you do is kiss, and she doesn't even really know what that is, either. Her mother was even less informative than Mrs. Bradshaw."

"Then she can talk to her sisters. She has three of them and they are all married. I'm sure Mary would set her straight."

"Of course, so I told her." This was at least partially true. "Anyway, I told her it was nice."

"Nice? That should reassure her!" he said with a chuckle. "Hmm... let's see how *nice* it can be..."

He threw himself upon her and kissed her fiercely.

"Lysander!" protested Sophy, laughing. "Bully me if you like, but I shall have my revenge when you see the enormous bill from Marianne. And, by the way, as a married bridesmaid, I shall have to wear a lace cap. I shall look like your grandmother."

He burst out laughing. "But my grandmother was... quite pretty," he said, "... for an older woman!" He rolled onto his back. "A lace cap, by God!" He laughed and laughed

CHAPTER EIGHT

In which Lord and Lady Hale host a wedding

Charles and Georgianna were married on a beautiful day towards the end of May. The London parks were pink and white with the blossom of fruit trees and the smell of lilac was in the air. Even the streets were less muddy than usual. While Charles and Lysander went to St. George's Church, Hanover Square, Sophy went to Aunt Mildred's townhouse to pick up Georgianna and her parents in the Hale Coach, the same one she had travelled to the church in for her own wedding. It was an enormously dignified affair. The coach was drawn by four matched black horses with plumes. The doors were emblazoned with the Hale H in a gold script, beneath which was a shield displaying on a field of green a black eagle, wings spread, with golden claws and tongue bearing the motto *Potentia et Honor* – the blazon of the House of Hale. There was a coachman and postilion in front and two grooms behind, all wearing livery. Aunt Mildred preened herself as the grooms, having lowered the steps, handed her down outside the Church.

Whether her husband's aunt was wearing a new dress was hard for Sophy to judge, since she rarely saw her at public events. It was not in the style of three years ago when Mary was married, nor yet in the style of the day. It neither hung straight from beneath the bosom nor was the bodice fitted. It was an indeterminate shape with fairly wide skirts in a stripe of red and gold. The best that could be said for it was that it looked comfortable. Mildred had chosen a high-crowned bonnet with a very wide brim and red and gold feathers. Luckily, the top of the Hale coach was quite high and the banquettes were wide, so there was enough space. Since Georgianna's father was slim, and the bride petite, wearing a veil instead of a bonnet, they could sit on one side. Sophy, wearing the much-dreaded lace cap, could fit beside Lysander's aunt.

In fact, the lace cap looked very pretty. It had been made of the same lace as her overdress. Susan had taken one look at it and gathered Sophy's curls onto the top of her head. She pinned the lace cap over them, then released curls through the lace in careful disorder all around. The effect was charming. Lysander had not seen it yet, as he had left Hale House to pick up Charles before she was down. But when he saw her later, he declared in a low voice that she should never wear anything else, or better still, wear nothing else.

The wedding service was lovely, as they always are when the bride and groom are young, in love and good-looking. Sylvester caused a brief titter of amusement when, instead of walking behind the bride, he decided he wanted to walk in front and scatter the "fowers" with the little maiden thus engaged. Throwing handfuls of rose petals violently left and right amused him immensely until his father caught his eye and frowned at him so severely that he immediately retired to his proper place.

The bride looked lovely in her simple but elegant pale pink gown. The color complemented her fairness and the natural blush of her cheeks. Sophy thought again what talent Marianne had in the choice of color and style. For his wedding, Charles had adopted none of the padded shoulder and wasp-waisted fashion of the young bucks, and he had no need to. His swallowtail grey superfine coat and trousers fit his muscular form to perfection and his new boots by Hoby shone like a mirror. His white starched shirt had a moderately high collar and Lysander himself had supervised the arrangement of his snowy neckcloth that morning. But it was his waistcoat that caught the eye. When Georgianna had said her gown was pale pink with a darker pink trim, he had had his tailor contact Marianne and use the same materials for his waistcoat, with the result that he had a waistcoat of alternating pink vertical stripes. It was a triumph. When the bride and groom stood together it made a remarkable effect.

Sophy herself was pleased with her new gown, for although pink was not really her color, Marianne had muted it with the overdress in an ivory that suited her skin tone. With the cap and her curls, she looked a ridiculously young matron. When he saw her, his lordship's eyes lit up and he gave her his wonderful smile.

Virginie Beaufort was in the pews. She saw the wordless exchange and ground her teeth. She had made a disastrous mistake in rejecting Lysander when he first proposed a liaison, thinking he would ask her again, and she would be able to make her own terms. But by then he had met Sophy. Then she had had a very brief affair with Charles and was not quite sure why it had ended, but ended it had. Then for some time she had enjoyed a flirtation with the Prince of Wales, but once he became King, he had quickly dropped her. She was currently between lovers, though Bunny Joliffe had been paying her marked attention of late. Pity he was married, but he might do for the time being.

The wedding breakfast was at Hale House, where the dining table had been expanded to its maximum of forty covers. The family on both sides accounted for a little over half that number. Charles' father was too ill to attend, a fact which cast a certain pall on the proceedings until the effects of his lordship's excellent champagne began to be felt. Then the younger set, including Charles' younger brother David and other unmarried friends of the bride and groom began to entertain and flirt with each other. As will usually happen in such situations, their voices grew louder and more cheerful. Some of them had not been to Hale House before and the painted ceilings and walls attracted a good deal of comment. The half-naked nymphs and their flute-playing attendants dining al fresco above their heads gave rise to several scandalous suggestions for picnics, causing rosy blushes from the young ladies. Sophy reflected that though she was not much older than most of them, she felt very matronly. So perhaps the cap was not so inappropriate after all.

The meal was the best that money could buy. Quite apart from the fact that Georgianna was a family member, the Earl would have spared no expense for Charles, his best friend. Early strawberries and raspberries had been sent up from the Court hot houses, together with spring lamb, poultry and vegetables. Mrs. Wilkins and Sophy had put their heads together to decorate the hall with pink roses and gardenias, whose perfume scented the whole house. On the dining table were huge blossoms of pink and white peonies, cut low along the length of the whole table, interspersed with silver candelabra. It was simple, but beautiful. Aunts Dorothea and Mildred tut-tutted over the obvious expense of it all and shook their heads, but that did not stop them from fully enjoying all that was on offer.

The meal took its usual course and just before the serving of the traditional bride's pie, his lordship rose to make the toast.

"It is no secret," he said, "that Charles Alverstoke and I have been friends for a very long time." He paused, then carried on to almost continuous laughter, "My first memory is of a terrified boy on our first day at Eton, wearing itchy wool knickerbockers and crying for his Mama. That was me. Charles was perfectly calm, bouncing a tennis ball he apparently kept in his pocket at all times. Luckily, they put us in the same House, so naturally we formed a bond. We had a good alliance. I learned to read Horace and he learned to kick a ball with devastating accuracy. I learned to do geometry and he learned to flirt with the housemaids. I learned Greek and he learned where we could buy oysters and white wine for a shilling. If you say that he spent his time more profitably, you are probably right. Since we grew to man's estate, he has certainly lived a more... let us say, colorful life than I. If ever there is a group organizing a sporting event, no matter how extraordinary, Charles is certainly in the midst of it, wearing one of the sober waistcoats he is famous for. Riding a horse backwards to Highgate, putting a goose in bed with a Councilman, and consuming an inhuman amount of jellied eels in a contest in Cheapside spring immediately to mind, though there are many, many more, most not suitable for mixed company."

He stopped for a moment for the laughter to die down before looking directly at his friend. "But I can also say," he continued seriously, "that if ever you need help, Charles will be there. If ever you need someone to do you a favor, Charles will be there. If ever you need a friend, and I most certainly have, Charles will be there. I know he will be a good husband to my cousin Georgianna, and because she is not only a sweet, beautiful girl, but also a sensible one, she will be an excellent wife for him. It is too much to hope she will be able to control his sartorial excesses, for many have tried and many have failed, but I am sure she will add to his happiness, and I know he will add to hers. He is the best man I know and I am honored to welcome him into the family. Ladies and gentlemen, please be upstanding for the Honorable and Mrs. Charles Alverstoke."

The assembled guests rose to their feet to drink the toast. Charles wrung his friend's hand and gripped his shoulder, and his lordship bent down so that Georgianna could kiss him on the cheek. The bride's pie was cut and eaten, and, to loud acclaim, Charles' sister Delia found the ring. Everyone looked at his lordship's secretary James Mead, and several of the younger set clapped him on the back. This young man had begun to pay Delia marked attention. She was just like her brother, full of fun and hardly ever serious. James was just the opposite, a studious young man, preparing for what he hoped would be a career in politics. They seemed an unlikely couple, but each tempered the character of the other, and those who knew them, like Lord and Lady Hale, thought the match very fine indeed.

Georgianna went up to Sophy's bedchamber where Susan helped her into her new travelling dress and the happy pair set out for the trip to Italy. The wedding breakfast broke up, with Aunt Mildred asking his lordship to call the Hale coach for herself and her husband.

"We came in it, after all," she said, "and it would take too long for us to summon our own carriage now."

Faced with the prospect of having to entertain his aunt while she awaited her own carriage, his lordship readily agreed, and told Pennyworth to send word to the stables. Aunt Dorothea sniffed and muttered something about encroaching relations, but Mildred was too pleased with herself to take any notice.

After seeing the last of the guests from the house, my lord and lady went up to the nursery to see the heir. They came in the door to the sound of him shouting, "Vester Barrington will 'tect you, arrgh!" and saw him running with his wooden sword at the paper shape of a man hanging from the ceiling.

"Papa! Mama!" cried Sylvester. "Daisy finded my sword! Look what she cutted with scissors! And I killed him!"

"Look at that, my lady," said his father, "we have a *veray parfit gentil knight* to protect us. We need have no fear." He swept a bow to his son, "Sir Sylvester, I thank you." Then he continued, "Why don't you go down the kitchen, Sir Sylvester, and see if there are any strawberries left from the party? In fact, let's all go down."

His lordship swung his son onto his shoulders and went swiftly to the stairs, where he ran down to the kitchen, bouncing Sylvester all the way, to his son's screaming delight.

In her husband's bed later that night, for the flowered bower bed in her room was still out of commission, Sophy took his head in her hands and kissed him tenderly.

"It makes me sad to think of you going off to school and crying for your Mama," she said.

"If thinking of it encourages you kiss me like that, I hate to disabuse you," he replied, "but it was poetic license. I didn't cry for my Mama. I never saw much of her, you know, as I was at the Court and she was in London most of the time. If anything, I cried for Cook. You know how I love her almond pastries! Matter of fact I was glad to be going away to school. My old tutor was a bore and I'd read all the books."

"Oh, Lysander, you are such a sham! But it was a lovely speech and you looked so handsome I couldn't bear it. I felt the way I did when I first saw you. You were easily the handsomest man in the room." She kissed him lightly. "And the cleverest." She kissed him again. "And the most desirable." She kissed him a third time.

"Pity I don't have more friends to marry off if this is the reaction it gets," murmured her husband in her ear. "But I don't believe you were so attracted to me when you first saw me. You were haughty and distant, as I remember. But I know how I felt, and I regard it as the irrefutable proof of being a gentleman that I didn't ravish you right there and then."

"I was so confused," she answered. "I didn't understand myself. I wanted to dislike you because I knew somehow you weren't being straightforward, but I had the oddest sensation when you looked at me. I know now what it was. I wanted you. I wanted you desperately, just as I've wanted you ever since, even when I was really vexed with you. So if you feel like ravishing me now, I won't put up any resistance."

He did, and she did not.

CHAPTER NINE

In which her ladyship has regrets

It was only two weeks after the wedding when an urgent message was sent to Venice, where the newlyweds were staying at the Ca' Foscari Palace, to say that Charles' father was near to death. They should return to London with all possible haste. The couple arrived in London five days later, and Charles was able to be by the bedside as his father died.

Although long expected, this event meant difficulties for everyone. Charles' mother knew her daughter-in-law should now take her place in the London family house. But it had been her home all these years, and both Charles and Georgianna were too softhearted to insist upon her immediate removal to the Dower House in the country. Furthermore, it would be an extreme hardship for Delia, who was still unmarried and would have to go with her mother, to leave London now that James Mead might be close to making a declaration. In tears, she declared her Papa had loved her and she was sure he would not have wanted to blight her entire future happiness by moving to the country. It was true that the late Baron Alverstoke had adored his youngest daughter and would probably have urged her to stay where she was happy.

So Charles and his mother decided they would all remain quietly where they were. The newlyweds would stay in the Park Street house Charles had rented. In truth, Georgianna was so happy to be mistress of her own establishment, and so in love with Charles, that she would have been happy anywhere.

During the first six months of mourning, it would not be appropriate for them to go to any gatherings except with close family. Georgianna would be expected to wear black during that time, but after that period she could go into half-mourning of lavender or grey. Charles would wear dark coats with a black armband and for the first time in his adult life, abandon his highly-colored waistcoats for black ones. He looked quite unlike himself.

The only place the newlyweds went to after the funeral was Hale House. Though Charles greeted them both with his usual friendliness, Sophy thought he seemed a little cooler to her than usual. She put it down to his having lost his father so recently. He certainly made them laugh over dinner, describing how he tried to explain their dinner orders in Italian.

"First I simply added 'o' to English words and waved my arms around, but we got fish instead of wine and chops instead of cheese," he laughed, "so then I just walked from table to table pointin' at what other people had. They knew I was an Englishman, so they made allowances, don't you know!"

"With your waistcoats and your gibbering, I daresay they thought you were a madman," remarked his lordship, dryly.

"But he was so clever, and after that, we always got what we wanted!" said Georgianna with an admiring look at her new husband. "And when we left, everyone came out to say goodbye. I think they were sorry to see us go, but of course, neither of us could understand a word!"

When the ladies left the gentlemen to their port, Georgianna could hardly wait for the door to shut behind Pennyworth before she said,

"Oh Sophy, I'm so glad you had me talk to Marianne before my wedding night! It made everything so much easier. I think Charles was glad too, though he didn't say anything."

She talked on excitedly about their trip and Charles, and how wonderful he was, and how much she liked being married, until the men came in. Unusually, they were not laughing as they came into the drawing room, but, again, Sophy attributed it to the recent death in the family. Charles both looked different in his black waistcoat and seemed changed in himself. Sophy found herself missing their old friend, and hoped it was not permanent.

"Georgianna is very happy," remarked Sophy as she and her husband lay together that night.

"Hmm, yes," responded his lordship, "but I need to speak to you about that, my love."

"Oh dear," replied Sophy turning to face him. "What is it?"

"Charles tells me you took Georgianna to see Marianne to talk about... marital relations. Is this so?"

"I didn't take her to Marianne *only* for that. You know she had her wedding clothes made by her."

"Don't prevaricate, Sophy. Did you, or didn't you?"

"Yes, I did."

"But I remember when you mentioned her ignorance, I suggested she talk to her sisters. I thought you agreed. Why did you go to Marianne?"

"It was too late. We had already been by then. Perhaps her sisters would have been better, but I doubt it. She told me this evening that what Marianne said was really useful. So what's the matter? I talked to Marianne and you weren't cross. Quite the opposite!"

"It's not the same thing. You were already... experienced when you talked to her. We had been married about three months. I'm not cross, but Charles is, or at least, as cross as he's capable of being. The trouble is that from the first time they were... together, he has had to hear the refrain 'Marianne says...' and it's making him very uncomfortable. He has my deepest sympathies! Sophy, Charles is not unfeeling, you know he isn't! He is quite capable of showing Georgianna how to go on, just as I showed you."

"You think women should come into marriage utterly ignorant so that their lord and master should have the pleasure of *showing them how to go on*? How wonderful for you all, to be sure!" cried Sophy, indignantly. "Women aren't children! We have the right to know what to expect!"

Her husband sighed. "You cannot interfere in people's lives like this my love, no matter what you think women's rights may be! You effectively spoiled Charles' wedding night!"

"But not Georgianna's, she told me so! And as far as Charles is concerned, I'm sure you are refining too much upon it. I shall ask him myself!"

"Sophy! I forbid you! You will do no such thing. Good Lord! It's above enough that he has Marianne in his bed, he doesn't need you too!"

"Don't be ridiculous, Lysander! Charles loves me and he won't mind if I talk to him."

"He will be horrified! I mean it, Sophy! You are not to say anything to him. I absolutely forbid it."

"Stop treating me like a child! You cannot forbid me to speak my mind. This is the nineteenth century, not the Middle Ages!"

"Now you *are* making me cross!" said her husband with heat. "I can and do forbid you to speak your mind in such a case as this. It is not your business to speak to Charles. He would not thank you for it. I expect you to do as I say, Sophy. Look at me and promise."

Sophy looked at her husband. "'Look at me and promise?'" she mimicked, equally angrily. "You, like all men, think women are children. You are talking to me just as you would to Sylvester. I shall not promise any such thing!" She got down from her husband's high bed and stalked into her own room.

The next day my lord and lady treated each other with a cool civility that was quite unlike their usual loving way. Sophy spent the morning trying to interest Sylvester in painting with her, to no avail. He could not wait to get back to his sword. After lunch, she called for her carriage, and left, not saying where she was going. His lordship closeted himself in his office and read Marcus Aurelius in Greek, soon becoming absorbed. His annoyance with his wife dissolved. She returned just before teatime and swept in the front door, her chin up, daring anyone to ask where she had been. Pennyworth merely enquired whether she had spent an agreeable afternoon and asked if she had had tea.

"No," she replied, "and I should very much like some. Have it brought to my room, if you please."

Hearing her return, her husband, his temper much improved, emerged from his office just as Sylvester, with Daisy running after him, came barreling down the stairs, crying, "I killed him and he fell down and he gots a big hole! Mama, Papa, he falled down with a big hole!"

It appeared that the paper figure, after a number of severe attacks, had torn apart and given up the ghost.

"Never mind," said his father. "I daresay Daisy can make you another. Or perhaps Mama will paint one for you." He raised one eyebrow at her.

"I'm going upstairs to take off my bonnet and pelisse and have a cup of tea," responded Sophy, pretending to ignore him.

"Oh dear," said her husband, giving the downcast look so like his son's when refused something he wanted, that she had to struggle not to laugh, "Mama is vexed with me. You'd better come up with me, Sylvester, to protect me."

"I 'tect you, Papa," said his son, gamely. "But I don't gots my sword!"

"I don't think you need your sword to protect me from your Mama. You're not going to make a hole in her, I think! Come on, let's go up. Perhaps Mama will share her tea with us."

"I don't yike tea, Papa!"

"I'm glad to hear it, neither do I! I hope that means you have a good palate. I look forward to sharing a bottle of your grandfather's brandy with you when you're older. Your mother thinks it's horrible."

"I yike bandy, Papa!"

"Good man!" and they followed her ladyship upstairs together.

Sophy had heard this exchange and smiled. It was impossible to be vexed with her husband for long, but she was determined not to give in too easily. A maid had brought her tea, together with some of the small cakes they all liked. When Sylvester saw them, he was going to make a dash for the plate, but his Papa held him back.

"Wait, Sylvester! Did Mama invite you to have a cake?"

The child shook his head.

"So, what must you say?"

"Peese Mama, I have a cake?"

"Of course, my darling. But why don't you first offer one to your Papa. He likes them too." Sophy forgot all about giving in too easily.

"Papa, you yike a cake?" said the little boy, holding out the plate at such an angle that all its contents were in danger of landing on the carpet.

"Thank you, Sylvester," replied his father, rescuing the plate. "I will have one, but not before your Mama." He offered the plate to his wife with his charming smile.

All resolution gone, Sophy took one and handed it to her son.

"This is a game that can go on forever," she said, "handing cakes to each other. Someone has to have the first, and it shall be you, Sylvester, for being such a polite little boy and protecting your Papa so well."

Sylvester beamed, his mouth full of cake. Sophy drank her tea and then began unhooking the front of her gown.

"Why you gettin' your gown off, Mama?" asked her son, curiously.

"I have to get changed for dinner, and I'm a little tired. I thought I might lie down for a while," responded her ladyship, looking directly at her husband, who raised an eyebrow.

Luckily, Daisy appeared at the open door. She bobbed a curtsey.

"Cook says Sylvester's supper is on the table, m'lady," she said, "and she don't want it to get cold. May I take him down now?"

"You 'sposed to say 'she *doesn't* want it to get cold', Daisy," corrected the young lord, going to her, and added, "Mama says." Then he remarked, leaving the room with her, "I gots cheese pudding for supper. I very yike cheese pudding!"

"I very yike cheese pudding too," murmured the Earl, closing the bedroom door and taking his wife in his arms, "But there are other things I very yike even more."

"Wait!" said his wife, holding him off. "Before we talk about what you like more than cheese pudding, I'd better tell you that I went to see Georgianna this afternoon, and I saw Charles too."

"Sophy!" her husband stiffened and gave an exasperated sigh.

"You didn't say I couldn't speak to Georgianna, and I didn't really speak to Charles… much." She hurried on. "Luckily Charles was out when I arrived, so I saw Georgianna alone. I told her what you had told me, well, more or less, and told her to stop mentioning Marianne. I explained that gentlemen need to feel totally in charge when they're… well, you know."

She thought for a moment, then continued, "I said it's much better to tell them how wonderful they are, and make them think everything is their idea. Men are just little boys, like Sylvester with his cake. You just have to tell them what they want to hear. You wouldn't think I'd even have to say it, it's obvious! When I think of the times I've had to dance with the odious Prince Regent, now an equally odious King! Why, all he wants is for you to say how marvelous he is, how he knows such clever steps, and you are just a poor woman trying to keep up with him, when in fact one is perpetually trying to avoid having him tread on one's toes. All men are the same, in need of constant admiration."

Lysander laughed a little ruefully. "So that is what you think of us! And that is what you said to Georgianna?"

"Yes, well, most of it. Of course, she saw the sense in what I was saying. She's not stupid, even though I must say that mentioning Marianne at every tiff and turn was quite silly, and so I told her. Charles will have no more complaints. She will puff up his pride no end and he will think he's a god amongst men! She really does love him, you know, and only wants to please him. I met him on the doorstep just as I was leaving and I said I was very sorry to have been so interfering, and I only meant it for the best and I hoped we could be friends again. He was most affected. You know how inarticulate he gets! But he kissed my hand and my cheek, so I think he forgave me."

"I'm sure he did. He is the stoutest fellow alive and never bears a grudge. I'm glad you apologized to him, Sophy, even though I told you not to speak to him. You chose the best course. Thank you."

Then after a moment he continued in a different tone, "So, you think us all little boys and yet Georgianna will make Charles think he's a god amongst men. Is that your view of me too?" He kissed her breast, where her gown was unhooked.

"Of course, Lysander," she replied, ruffling the top of his head, answering only one half of the question and glad he could not see her indulgent smile. "Sylvester certainly thinks you're a god, and so do I."

"Then this god would like his handmaiden to remove all her garments and arrange herself upon the couch in her bower," said her husband. "He will do the same and celestial forces will do the rest."

"Will it be heaven?"

"Most definitely."

Afterwards they both lay dozing until Sophy said, "We should get ready to go down. We are invited to the Ranelaghs' tonight, remember."

"Oh God! Not Ned Ranelagh. He's bound to want to play cards after dinner and it'll be hard to lose. He's a pitiful player but one can't fleece one's host. Let's send a note to say we are both indisposed and just stay here."

"You know we cannot do that."

"I'm the Earl and a god. I should be able to do what I want."

"No," said Sophy, "you are just Mr. Barrington, with family responsibilities and a nag of a wife. Sorry, but there it is." She pushed him out of the bed, which creaked in protest.

"I'm going to have this damned bed chopped up for firewood!" he declared, grabbing up his clothes and going towards the communicating door. "I, the Earl, have spoken!"

Sophy laughed as he opened the door. "Whatever his lordship commands," she said, and then as the door closed, "just a big little boy!"

CHAPTER TEN

In which her ladyship gives away a painting

Sophy had finished painting the sketches done in the park during the weeks before Charles' wedding. They were a collection of tulips, late jonquils and rhododendrons with the suggestion of fruit tree blossoms in the background. The little pictures had just come back framed by the house carpenter.

"Oh, my lady! They're so pretty!" said Susan when she saw them all laid out on her ladyship's desk.

"Please choose one for yourself, if you would like," said Sophy. "But if you please, not the rhododendron one, as I have it in mind for a friend."

Knowing that her mistress always gave away the majority of her little paintings, Susan gratefully accepted the offer and said, "Then, if you don't mind, my lady, I'll take the tulips. I love them. They're like us women, don't you think? Upright and tall with their skirts pulled tight when they're young, then more and more open in middle age like they was opening their laps for their children and grandchildren, until they gets old and drooped and blousy, but still lovely. Like my old Gran!"

"Susan, you are a poet!" cried Sophy, much impressed. "Now that you say it, I see you are absolutely right. I shall never think of tulips the same again. How clever you are!" She thought for a moment. "You know, I don't think I've ever met your grandmother. I hope I may see her this summer."

Over the last four years, Sophy had met most of Susan's family during their summer months at Hale Court. It was practice for the London servants to come from the Court, so they nearly all had family back in the country. Susan's two brothers, about whom she often talked, had stayed on the farm, but they had once at, Sophy's invitation, come up to Hale House. Susan had laughingly remarked how they would love the painted ceilings and walls because of the practically bare-breasted maidens cavorting everywhere with their rosy bottoms easily discernible through their diaphanous robes.

When they first saw the public rooms they stood, their eyes gazing wonderingly upwards, mouths open, twisting their caps in their hands, until Susan told them sharply to make their bow to her ladyship, who had come in to greet them. Sophy would have loved to stay and talk, because if they were anything like their sister, they would make her laugh. But she could see that her presence inhibited them, so after telling them to be sure to make a good dinner in the servants' hall, where Cook was expecting them, she left them to their gazing. She could hear their comments once she had left the room.

"Blimey!" said one, "Imagine what Dad would say if you was to float around in the woods like that with your bum and the rest all showing!"

"Not too good if you was to sit on some nettles, neither!" said the other, snorting with suppressed laughter.

"It's Art, you idiots," said Susan, who by now had been to numerous galleries with her ladyship and was quite used to representations of the naked female form. "It's the imagination of the artist. It's not supposed to be real!"

"Cor, some imagination, this one's got," replied her brother, still snorting, "It's a wonder he can sleep at night."

"He don't sleep!" added the other, in convulsions. "He's got too much of a stiffy!"

"If you carry on like that, I'll put you out in the street and you'll miss your dinner," Susan reprimanded them severely. "What if her ladyship was to hear you… or his lordship," she added with a slight tremble, for like Sylvester, she did regard the Earl much as a god. Although he was unfailingly polite to her, she was rather afraid of him.

Of course, had she but known it, Lysander would have agreed with her brothers. His mind often dwelled pleasurably on the thought of a rosy bottom and a full bosom, and so he told his wife when she laughingly reported this conversation to him.

"Then you are an idiot, too!" said Sophy. "It's Art!"

"It certainly is," his lordship responded, putting his arms around her and cupping her buttocks in his hands. "And it's my private collection!"

Sophy had decided that she would give the rhododendron watercolor to Sally Joliffe. She told herself it was out of simple friendship and because that lady had so admired the sketch, but she knew in her heart that it was because she was still curious about Sally's involvement with her husband. She had sent a note asking if she might drop by one afternoon and this was the chosen date. Accordingly, she set forth after lunch to the Joliffe mansion. This turned out to be very close, on Park Lane.

Sally Joliffe greeted her graciously but, Sophy thought, a little warily. However, once tea had been served, the purpose of the visit revealed, and the little painting handed over, her hostess lost her restraint and became much warmer.

"Why, it is even prettier than I remember," she said in the musical voice Sophy remembered from their meeting in the park.

"Well", she said, "it always looks better when it's painted, as I think I told you, but thank you, I'm glad you like it."

"I'm particularly fond of rhododendrons," said Sally, half to herself. "They always remind me of..." but she seemed to collect herself and finished, in a brisker tone, "of... where I grew up."

Sophy was quite sure that was not what Sally was going to say, but she replied, in the same tone, "And where was that? Where did you grow up?"

"In the country. My family home is in Devizes, in Wiltshire. I am from the Vyse family, which, according to family history, has been there forever. My father was the Marquis of Colne." Sally Joliffe continued in her lovely voice. "I was rarely in London before my coming out. Oh, I was so excited to be coming here! I stayed with my Aunt, Lady Bourne, who is dead now, God rest her soul. I was presented at Court, of course, and wore a white dress with short sleeves and a long train. My goodness, what trouble I had with that train! You were supposed to hold it over your arm until the actual presentation to the king, but either mine was too long, or I'm too short, but I couldn't get it just right! I'm sure I looked a perfect fright, with the three white feathers in my hair, too! White has never been my color anyway! But after that I went to all the balls and parties! It was so much fun!" She sat for a moment, with a far-away look in her eye.

"I shouldn't say it, I know," she finally continued, "but I was a great success. Of course, I was much prettier than I am now."

Sophy made a small sound of protest for, indeed, Sally Joliffe was still a pretty woman.

But her hostess carried on, "and I was less... there was less of me than there is now. Oh, my dear!" she burst out, "you are so lucky to be tall and slender! I am sure you will never put on weight! I have always been one of those small, round people, you know, inclined to corpulence. I'm sure that's why my husband... after Ruth was born..." Her voice faded again.

"Did you meet your husband in your first Season?"

"Yes. He noticed me right away and was always the first to put his name on my dance card. His attention was most marked. He sent me flowers and gifts. The doorbell was forever ringing! My aunt warned me not to form an attachment too quickly, and said I should wait a little, but he was so handsome and charming! To be sure, his family was not quite as... well, not of quite the same rank as mine, but I couldn't help falling in love with him. He is a little older than I and has always lived in London. He seemed so... worldly, and, looking back, I see now that I was such an innocent."

Then she seemed to collect herself. "But why am I chattering on like this, we are hardly acquainted, and all this is ancient history, it must be such a bore for you!"

"Not at all," cried Sophy. "Indeed, I know what you mean about being an innocent. I'm sure you know I was a country girl myself. I had never been to London till Lysander brought me here after our wedding."

"Ah! Lysander! I'm sure Lysander was kindness itself!" said Sally. "I know he..." and she abruptly stopped.

"Do you know my husband well?" asked Sophy quickly, feeling she had at last come to the issue. I didn't know you were a close friend of his."

Sally Joliffe blushed violently. "Oh!" she stammered. "Oh! Know him well? At one time... that's to say... I knew him... at one time..." She seemed incapable of continuing.

Sophy leaned forward and clasped her hostess's trembling hands.

"Dear Mrs. Joliffe... Sally," she said gently, "dear Sally, let me say that I believe you were at one time... intimate with him. Please forgive me, I do not say this to distress you. I don't mean to hurt you in any way. I should not be talking to you about this at all, and I know Lysander would be furious if he knew. But I want to know! I just want to know! Everyone says he had a number of *chères amies*, and of course, no one knew me at all before we were married. I had never been in London in my life. Whenever we go to assemblies or balls, people still make comments behind their hands. Is it so wrong of me to want to know what they know?"

"I suppose not," said Sally, in her low voice. "Though everyone knows he's never looked at another woman since he married you. It's much worse when the indiscretions take place... when one is married." She was quiet for a moment, then with determination, she continued, "I'm going to tell you something I've never told anyone. I did have a liaison with your husband. He wasn't Lord Hale then. He was Lysander Barrington, and he was the most charming man I had ever, and have ever, met. I had been married just under two years and by then I knew my husband's interest was... well, to be frank, he was at least as much attached to my fortune as to myself. I told you my family was of a higher rank than his. My fortune was substantial."

She stopped, then gathering herself together, continued, "even before I had Ruth, he had a number of attachments, one after the other, and I was so miserable. When I did not give him a son, he began to ignore me almost totally. One evening, Lysander was seated next to me at a dinner party and he made me laugh. I had felt I would never laugh again. And that wonderful smile! I saw him a few days later at a ball, and we danced. You know what a good dancer he is! Then during a carriage ride in the park, he drew up beside me on his horse. The rhododendrons were in bloom. I still think of him whenever I see them. We... began our affair that day. We were very discrete and I didn't think anyone knew. How did you know? Who told you?"

"Oh, no one in particular," replied Sophy, not very truthfully. "I really didn't know, it was a suspicion. You have my word that I shall never tell anyone what you have told me."

"Thank you." Sally thought again. "I may as well say that it only lasted a few weeks. I was a young mother and the strain of clandestine meetings was just too great. I was so fearful Bunny would find out and he is so jealous, in spite of his own infidelities. I knew he would call Lysander out if he knew, so I ended it. But I've never regretted it. He made me happy and he was a perfect gentleman throughout. I'm sure you know how lucky you are."

"I do," said Sophy, in all sincerity. "May I ask you just one thing more? Did you ever hear anything about any other women and Lysander? I just want to know, that's all!"

"Well, there was Lizzy Ponsonby. There was a terrible scandal with her later. Nothing to do with Lysander. Something about her husband challenging Henry Guilfoyle to a duel. I don't know exactly what happened but Henry left town and Aubrey sent her to their place in the country. It was all ages ago! You must know that Lysander was interested in a number of other women over the years. But I never heard of him chasing after unmarried girls. They were all either widowed or had complaisant husbands. That's how it was, well, still is, you know. Many couples live quite separate lives and... entertain other people. So long as they are reasonably discrete, no one thinks anything of it. Of course, Prinny – the Prince Regent as he used to be – quite set the standard in that regard!"

"Yes, I see." Sophy thought for a moment and then continued, "I hope you won't think it disloyal if I say I really do not like the Prince, or the King, as he is now. Of course, he is our Monarch and I respect that, but as a man I find him quite horrid! I suppose he has always been very much indulged, but really, why he should have such a high opinion of himself is incomprehensible! He is in no way good looking and his manners are all puff and consequence. Yet he appears to think that all women must fall at his feet! He has even tried to flirt with me occasionally, though how he could possibly imagine I could be interested in his attention when I am married to such a man as Lysander, is quite beyond me!"

Sally Joliffe laughed. "Oh, my dear! I find you so refreshing! What you are saying is what many of us think, but no one dares say! Of course, he was very good-looking when he was younger, and much less stout. Nowadays he positively creaks when he moves – his corsets, you know. Although I did hear his doctor has forbidden him to be so tightly laced. It was interfering with his digestion, apparently. But I'm ashamed to say, we did all fall at his feet when he was in his prime and I suppose he grew used to it. He was always very free with his hands, I must say, and one had to avoid him if one could. I remember Bunny being quite incensed on an occasion when the Prince adjusted a corsage I was wearing and put his hands on my bosom. But what could I do? One could not make a scene! That was in the early days of our marriage, of course."

She smiled wistfully and then sighed. "Ah, if one could have one's time over…" She did not finish the sentence, but rallied and said in a brighter tone, "But I am delighted to have had this opportunity to get to know you better, my dear Lady Hale… Sophy. I wish you every happiness and I cannot thank you enough for your gift. The rhododendrons will always remind me of you both."

It was clear that confidences were at an end, and soon after that, Sophy took her leave. She felt she had not only found out what she wanted to know but had also made a friend

CHAPTER ELEVEN

In which Lord and Lady Hale visit their friends, and Mr. Joliffe makes one

A week or so later, Lady Threlfall hosted another of her many social events during the season. Lord and Lady Hale had been invited but used the excuse of a previous engagement to cry off. In fact, they had been invited to a quiet dinner with Charles and Georgianna. The couple were still in mourning and not attending or holding large parties, which for Georgianna was a relief, since she felt unequal to anything more.

"How do you do it?" she asked Sophy, as they sat, head to head, while the men were enjoying a glass of sherry before dinner. "Even with just you two good friends coming, my peace has been quite cut up, and I cannot imagine a whole rout!"

They talked for some time about preparing for a large party, which Georgianna would have to do when she finally moved into Alverstoke Mansion, and which she was already regarding with foreboding.

"Don't give it a thought, Georgie," cried Charles when he heard what they were discussing. "I'll get some top of the trees cook and bottle washer to get it all done up to the nines, you see if I don't!"

Although Sophy still entertained doubts about Charles' abilities in these matters, Georgianna was reassured.

"He is so good to me," she said, looking at her husband adoringly. "He is a perfect husband and will never let me be troubled by anything. And his Mama has been so kind, even though she is so low at the moment."

They went into a dinner, which, if it was not quite perfect, was enjoyed with friendship and the best of good humor. After dinner, Georgianna asked her husband if it would be appropriate for them to play cards while still in mourning.

"Not to gamble, just… you know… for a little quiet entertainment," she said, "and I do so want Lysander to teach me to play piquet. When you explain it I get so confused."

"I'm not surprised," commented his lordship with a smile at his friend. "In the clubs they turn away when they see me coming, but they all love Charles. He's been known to pay a number of tailors' bills by his misfortune at cards."

"How unfair!" cried Sophy. "When I play with Charles, he beats me sometimes, and he doesn't try to distract me like you do!"

Lysander had taught his wife to play piquet in the early days of their marriage and she was now quite adept, though she rarely beat him. When she was trying to decide on her cards, he would look at her with such a suggestive expression, or give her his wonderful smile, and she would feel her blood rise and be unable to concentrate. She had once beaten him by distracting him as she gradually unhooked the front of her gown, and since then he had shown her no mercy.

Now he said, quite seriously, "What do you think, Charles? We're quite willing, but we will be guided by you."

"Well, the Pater liked a game of cards himself when he was in prime twig, so I don't think he would mind us playing," responded the man of the house.

Since piquet was a two-person game, Charles and Sophy played at one small table, while Lysander and Georgianna sat at another. Sophy could hear her husband's low, patient voice interspersed by his cousin's "Oh, I *see*!" while she and Charles played, albeit somewhat less riotously than usual. Their games were usually accompanied by much scoffing and crowing. She realized that there had been a change in their friend since the death of his father and his marriage. He still had his seemingly carefree way, but underneath, she detected a seriousness that had never been apparent before. Nonetheless, they had an enjoyable couple of games with their traditional wager: the loser had to kiss the winner on the cheek. As usual, kisses were exchanged, with accompanying exaggerated bows and curtseys.

When Georgianna saw this, she cried, "Oh, that's famous! I would never dare to kiss Lysander in the normal way! He has always scared me to death! Mama always said we had to be at our most ladylike when we visited Hale House."

"If the reports are true, dear cousin," replied his lordship, "then I am the only man in London you did not kiss when you were in your, let us call it, exuberant period."

"Such exaggeration!" protested the young wife. "It's true I was a little... unsteady, but I was never free with my kisses. Oh no, just the *promise* of my kisses!"

They all laughed and Charles said, "So long as from now on you promise to kiss only me, well, Sandy too, I suppose, if he beats you at cards, which," he added a little gloomily, "he will. I don't know how our friendship has lasted this long. I don't think I've ever beaten him, even when he was bosky!"

"It is how you repay me for the debts you incurred for all the prep I did for you at Eton," replied his lordship, "not to mention the scrapes I extricated you from at Oxford. But since we are in mixed company I will not go into details."

"Oh, do tell!" cried Georgianna. "I want something to hold over his head when he gets too high and mighty."

"High and mighty? Charles? Never!" declared Sophy with a laugh, though she thought
the new Charles might indeed deserve the description.

"Hmm, let's see..." considered his lordship. "Something I can repeat with ladies present. Well, he was, of course, a member of the Bullingdon Club, ostensibly to play cricket, but their behavior after the matches was notorious. After one such celebration, on his way back to his rooms, Charles conceived the idea of removing all the clothing from the Master of Balliol's chamber. How he did it, God only knows, for he was very drunk. But the Master was reputed to be a very heavy sleeper and Charles is, as we know, light on his feet. Anyway, all might have been well had he not also conceived of the idea of wearing some of the clothes, notably the disgusting old gown and mortarboard, to ride a donkey across the quad, right in front of the Master's windows, at about eleven the next morning. The uproar was immediate. The Proctor was called and Charles was hauled up before the Master."

"Who was still wearing his nightshirt, a revolting, stained old thing!" crowed Charles.

"But how did you explain it?" asked Sophy and Georgianna together.

"I went straight up to the Master," said Lysander, "and said I had found the clothes in a heap outside my door and, given their filthy, dilapidated state, assumed they had been left by a tramp who had slept there overnight. I said I had issued a general challenge, against a case of champagne, to anyone who would ride a donkey across the quad wearing them, and Charles took me up on it. And they believed me."

" 'Course they did," said Charles. "Sandy was everyone's pet - a scholar and a gentleman. He could natter in Latin with the best of 'em. Luckily, the Proctor didn't know I was his friend. That would have ruined his reputation!"

"The best of it was," continued his lordship, "I invited the Proctor to examine the clothing and tell me whether I could have possibly known it belonged to the Master. It was the most filthy, disreputable pile of rubbish. I swear he had had the gown since he was an undergraduate himself in the 1740's. And when the Proctor agreed with me, the Master was too ashamed to admit it was his and actually apologized to Charles!"

Both men roared with laughter at the memory. "And the Master was obliged to buy a new suit of clothes and a gown. He wore them for the rest of his life, as far as I know," laughed Lysander.

"And what happened to the donkey?" asked Sophy.

"Took him back to the farmer, 'course," said Charles, "but not before it ate everything in the quad flower beds!"

"I sent the Master the case of champagne I said I'd wagered," said Lysander, "with a quote from Marcus Aurelius that more or less translates as *It is man's peculiar duty to love even those who wrong him.* He knew he'd been fooled, but was man enough never to mention it again. Nice old duffer, actually."

The butler brought in the tea tray, and shortly after, Lord and Lady Hale took their leave. On their way home in the carriage, Sophy gave a sigh and moved close to her husband.

"They are so sweet together!" she said. "Did we look like that when we were first married?"

"You certainly looked sweet, my love," answered her husband, drawing her close, "but I hope I have never looked sweet in my life, and I don't think Charles would thank you for the description either!"

"You know what I mean," she rubbed her cheek on his shoulder. "They look so much in love. They are forever looking at each other and smiling."

"Ah, that is the effect of satisfactory carnal knowledge."

"Do you think so?"

"I'm sure so."

"Then my most recent advice must have worked!" said Sophy with satisfaction.

"Which advice would that be, my interfering minx?" responded his lordship with a chuckle. "The advice about flattering him? I don't think Charles is foolish enough to swallow that."

"You are mistaken, my lord. No man is proof against flummery of that sort in an intimate situation. That's something Marianne told me a long time ago and she should know."

At the Threlfal party the Hales had chosen not to attend, the Joliffes were amongst the many guests. Bunny was pleased when he saw Virginie Beaufort there. She was a taking little thing, not in her first youth, of course, and probably only five years younger than his wife, but much better preserved. To tell the truth, he was finding the younger women a little difficult these days. Only last week, he had lifted an eyebrow at a debutante and had been dismayed to see her look behind her to see for whom it might have been intended. She clearly did not think it was for herself. Later, he saw her talking to another young thing and make a small gesture towards him, giggling behind her fan. He could not understand it. He glanced at his reflection in the tall mirror behind him. He was still a fine figure of a man, wasn't he?

Virginie saw him look at her and gave him a coy smile. He made his way to her side. The gown she was wearing that evening was just to his taste. It had a low décolletage, revealing a good deal of her ample bosom. The bodice was fitted to just above her waist, from where the skirts fell in a V shape, but narrow over the hips and derrière. She was under middle height, but he had always preferred little women. He leaned over so that he could look down the front of her gown. Her white bosom was enhanced by a necklace of large rubies interspersed with pearls, and a matching pair of earrings hung from her lobes.

"Those rubies have never had a better resting place," he murmured.

Virginie glanced down and decided not to tell him that they had a been a gift from Lord Hale at the height of their flirtation. In fact, it was the gift of the rubies that had persuaded her he was seriously attached and she could afford to hold him off just a little longer. She had convinced herself she had the chance of being offered what she really wanted: the role of Countess to his Earldom. But she had mistaken her man. She shook off these unhappy thoughts and looked up into Bunny's florid countenance.

"Why, I thank you, sir," she answered in a low voice, "and since I know you are something of an expert in… er…. *resting places*, I am flattered."

Bunny was delighted with this response. It was exactly the sort of talk he could understand and indulge in.

"Even an expert can profit from further… investigation, my dear. I hope I may be afforded the opportunity."

"Perhaps, Mr. Joliffe," answered Virginie. "Perhaps."

Not wanting to make their tête-à-tête too obvious, she moved off to talk with some of the other guests. In truth, she did not have a great deal of interest in Bunny Joliffe. She did not think he would leave his wife, even though he obviously had ceased to care for her. Virginie's first husband had been a casualty of the Peninsular War, and she had been single for a little over five years. She had his military pension and some family money, but she had extravagant tastes, particularly in the matter of her wardrobe. She was at the point in her life when she needed a husband. Bunny was therefore a distraction, a possible source of expensive gifts, nothing more. The *on-dit* was that his wife was the one with the money, though the marriage settlements had been generous. But he was what was on offer at the moment, and she had learned a bitter lesson about delaying too long.

As she moved around the room, her eye was drawn to a small watercolor painting of the Threlfall front door hanging on the wall. She moved forward to look more closely at it and heard her hostess's voice at her side.

"Very nice, isn't it? Lady Hale, of course. She did it for me some weeks ago."

"I didn't know she was a particular friend of yours," murmured Virginie. Looking closely at the painting and seeing the SLH script signature in the corner, she suffered a pang, as she always did at the thought of Sophy.

"Well, we have become quite friendly. We had a long chat when she came to deliver the painting. We talked about the *ton* back when we were all, well, a little younger. She had never been to London before her marriage, you know, and wanted to know what it was like. She seemed particularly interested in Hale's... adventures. His light o' loves, you know."

"How diverting! Anyone of note? I must say, I would find that quite interesting too. I wasn't out then, of course." In this way, Virginie let her hostess know that there was, after all, some difference in their ages.

"Let's see, there was Maria Cholmeley, Suzie Oldkirk... Nell Greenwood, Prissy Westover, Alice Farley. There were so many, you know." Then, catching sight of Bunny Joliffe, who was still lingering quite close, she dropped her voice. "And there was that suspicion about Sally Joliffe, but no one ever really knew."

"Sally? No! Really?"

"As I say, no one ever really knew, but it's no secret Bunny only married her for her fortune and he had an affair before they were married a year, so...." She left the rest unsaid.

"Oh, these old stories!" Virginie smiled at her hostess. "Such fun! But I think I see…" She gave a little wave to no one in particular. "Excuse me, dear Lady Threlfall, such a delightful rout!" and she moved by a circuitous route back to Bunny Joliffe's side, thinking furiously about how she could turn this interesting information to her advantage.

"Bunny?" she said in a low voice, "If I may call you that?"

"You may call me anything you like if it will get me closer to those." He nodded towards her breasts.

"Then Bunny, would you like to pay me a call tomorrow afternoon around three? 17B Mount Street."

His already high color mounted. "By God! Would I? Three o'clock, you say? I'll be there!"

Virginie gave him a brief nod and moved away.

CHAPTER TWELVE

In which Virginie makes plans

Number 17B Mount Street was a charming little house tucked between two larger residences. It suited Virginie to perfection, being in a fashionable part of London yet because of its size, inexpensive to maintain. She could manage with few servants. She had dispensed with the service of a cook as she rarely ate a full meal in her own home. Her major domo could serve up a delightful little cold plate when required, and she made up with excellent wines what she did not offer in cuisine. Her gentlemen callers were always more than satisfied and indeed found her an excellent hostess.

She had married quite young and, her husband being a military man, she had become accustomed early to the company of men. She knew what they liked. She had not been faithful to her husband, nor he to her, and though she felt regret at his passing, it was more because life was indubitably easier as a married woman than as a widow.

After his death she had installed herself in London with a view to finding herself a new husband, if not at first, then surely at last. Her sitting room was arranged, one might say, for that purpose. It was charming but not overly feminine. It featured comfortable, ample chairs for her guests, with no spindly furniture a man might feel creaking beneath him. She had always encouraged snuff and more recently cigars, so a gentleman could sit at his ease and smoke. She kept up with the affairs of the day and took and read the important newspapers, so her callers could both read the news and, if they desired, discuss it with her. She could then flatter them on their superior knowledge. In this respect she and Sophy, not to mention Madame Marianne, would have been in agreement.

Those who were lucky enough to be invited into her boudoir found a far more feminine enclave. Her bed covers and hangings were dull pink satin, and the whole room was quite dark. It was illuminated day and night by candles set in front of gilt mirrors and perfumed by a pastille burner. Against the shadowy pink of the room, Virginie's soft white skin glowed and her doll-like beauty was seen at its best. To this she added a not inconsiderable expertise in the amorous arts. One might wonder why she had not managed to snare a suitable husband, since she was in many ways a perfect woman. The truth was, of course, that whereas many men were happy to enjoy her manifold qualities on a temporary basis, few were prepared to take on as a spouse a woman whose gifts, pleasurable as they might be, others had enjoyed as well.

When Bunny Joliffe, after a furtive look around him, knocked on the door of 17B Mount Street the following afternoon, he was led by her major domo into the comfortable sitting room. She greeted him wearing a modest, lace-edged white cotton lawn negligée tied with pink ribbons beneath her bosom. Over it she wore a fine, white cotton wrapper. It was her experience that men preferred this almost virginal look to something more daring. She herself poured him a glass of her excellent claret, her major domo having quietly disappeared. He drank it with as little attention as he might a glass of water, staring at her mostly concealed breasts. She offered him a cigar and asked him one or two questions about the affairs of the day, but he hardly heard her. Nevertheless, she deliberately kept him at arm's length until he growled,

"For God's sake, Virginie, let's get on with it!"

"My goodness, Bunny," she murmured, "you are impatient." She looked at him from under her lashes and then pouted, "But very well."

She led him into her bedchamber, turned to face him and removed her wrapper. He could hardly wait to undo the ribbons of her virginal nightgown and feel her nakedness beneath. He squeezed her breasts with a little more force than was comfortable and led her to the bed. She lay there while he removed his own clothing, wheezing at the effort. His boots gave him trouble, and Virginie wondered not for the first time, why, knowing that they would be needing to remove them, gentlemen wore boots to romantic assignations. They invariably went through the undignified contortions Bunny was performing now. At last he came to her, a corpulent figure with a mass of matted chest hair and a prominent stomach. He was evidently completely unaware of his own physical shortcomings and stood before her, *a fine figure of a man*, to use his own phrase.

He was not a skillful lover, in spite of having had many mistresses. Indeed, this never occurred to him. He was much more interested in his own pleasure than in that of his partner. Virginie did not need the advice Marianne had given to Sophy; she knew from experience that it was true. So she flattered his performance, clumsy though it was, simulating a pleasure she was far from experiencing. She told herself that, with time and if the plan she was hatching ended successfully, she could probably teach him to do better.

After this, to his mind, most successful interlude, Bunny enjoyed a second and third glass of claret, together with a cozy gossip about the shortcomings of mutual acquaintances. Virginie at last brought the conversation around to what she wanted to know.

"And your wife," Virginie asked, "is she understanding about your... lady friends? I should hate a scandal!" She lowered her eyes decorously.

"Oh, Sally? She's a good old thing," he replied nonchalantly. "Never says a word."

"And she doesn't... find solace elsewhere?"

"What? Good God, no!" he blustered. "And she'd better not! I'd have a short way with anyone who tried that, I can tell you!" He seemed surprised by the idea. "No, there's never been anything like that!"

The conversation continued on less personal lines, with Virginie asking several questions about political figures, questions to which, in truth, she knew the answers better than he. She sat next to him, occasionally patting him on the knee and agreeing with everything he said, so that by the time he departed, he thought her a most intelligent woman, as well as a damned attractive one.

When he finally left her, he went to his club with a spring in his step. Bunny's self-satisfied expression was not lost on other members and as the glasses of claret he had drunk at Virginie's were followed rapidly by several more, it was not long before his liaison with Virginie Beaufort was common knowledge.

It was not long, either, before Sally Joliffe heard about it, since there is never a shortage of persons who like to convey such news. In this case, it was a lady who passed as a friend and whose husband, like Sally's own, was known to entertain other women. Misery loves company.

"I don't know if you've heard," said that lady three or four days later, "and forgive me, my dear, if I speak out of turn, but I'm told Bunny has formed an attachment to a certain golden-haired widow of our acquaintance. I'm told he visits her in Mount Street every day."

Sally sighed. "I wondered if he might have found a new... friend," she said. "I have seen so little of him this last week. He is never at home."

Her heart dropped as she considered how much prettier than herself Virginie was, and what call on their purse this latest attachment might have. Virginie was known to have expensive tastes and was always beautifully gowned. She sighed again.

The question of calls on Bunny's purse was one that his new inamorata was also mulling over. The conversation after their first encounter had convinced Virginie that her new protector had no idea of his wife's infidelity in the early days of their marriage, and would probably react violently to it. She thought it unlikely Bunny would actually call out Hale, though the idea gave her a frisson of excitement. If he did, and actually killed the Earl, he would have to leave the country, which would suit her admirably. Virginie would go with him. As for Lysander, it would serve him and that oh-so-innocent wife of his right. But even if Bunny did not call Hale out, he might be enraged enough to leave his wife, especially if she made sure he was by that time besotted with herself. Divorce was almost impossible, and the best that could be hoped for was a Deed of Separation. She and Bunny would have to leave town, possibly to live in Paris for a while, until the circumstances of their relationship had been forgotten.

Was it worth it? she wondered. At the moment she was free to pursue her life as she wished. It would be otherwise with a husband or protector like Bunny, who would be jealous. But he was a man, and a member of the *ton*. He had the *entrée* everywhere and could be relied upon to deal with the annoyances of life: carriages, restaurant tables, tickets to the opera, sundry bills. Anyway, she thought, if she found someone better, she could always leave him. In the meantime, her dressmaker's bill was pressing, and her latest bonnet, as yet unpaid for, had cost a positive fortune. She felt confident she could convince Bunny to pay for these, particularly if she modelled her newest gown for him in private, or rather, the removal of it, and showed him the bonnet wearing nothing else at all.

It was with these thoughts in mind that over the next couple of weeks Virginie encouraged the attentions of Bunny Joliffe, using all the blandishments and amorous encouragement of a lifetime of practice. He became utterly infatuated with her and paid all her bills without a blink. Because of her constant admiration, he walked around like the cock of the roost, thinking himself a positive Casanova.

This was the state of affairs when the Joliffes went one evening to a rout given by Lady Burgess. Knowing Virginie would be there, Bunny had encouraged their early arrival and was then disappointed not to see her. He left his wife almost immediately and went into the card room where he drank several glasses of wine in quick succession. He recklessly played a few hands of cards and quickly lost more than he could afford. He wandered disconsolately back into the salon and brightened when he espied Virginie, who had just arrived, wearing the gown that had been modelled for him so deliciously. He went immediately to her side.

Lord and Lady Hale had arrived some time before, and Sophy had immediately seen Sally Joliffe sitting alone, looking around the room with a sad little smile on her pretty but careworn face.

"Oh, poor Sally Joliffe!" said Sophy in a low voice to her husband, indicating that lady with a slight nod of her head. "I expect you heard that her husband has been involved with Virginie Beaufort these last few weeks. It's such a shame!"

Lysander looked to where Sophy had nodded and saw Sally. Whether it was because of her brave smile, or the fact that his wife was by his side, he did something he had not done for years. After their affair, he had avoided Sally in public, only speaking to her in the company of others, and then exchanging the merest commonplaces. If he happened to catch her glance, he gave her the slightest smile and nod of a mere acquaintance, belied by the warmth in his eyes. Now, with his wife on his arm, he went directly to where she was sitting.

"Oh, Lady Hale... Sophy, and... my Lord," cried Sally, in some surprise. She raised herself slightly from her chair, as if to curtsey.

"Sally! Please stay where you are," said Sophy, "I'll take this chair next to you." She sat down. "What a frightful crush! I don't blame you for sitting apart. You will procure us a glass of lemonade, won't you, Lysander?"

Her husband said he would be delighted, bowed and left them.

"Sally, I haven't mentioned to Lysander that I know... anything," said Sophy urgently in a low voice. "I thought it best not to rake up old history."

"Of course, my dear. It is kind of you to approach me. I was so surprised. Lysander... his lordship... has been so discrete all these years."

The Earl returned with two glasses of lemonade, which he handed to the ladies, saying with a laugh, "I hope there is still something left to drink! I fear I may have spilled most of it making my way through the crowd. Why do we subject ourselves to this, I wonder? We could have a glass of lemonade at any time by our own fire in peace. Unless, of course, it is for the pleasure of seeing old friends." He turned his brilliant smile on Sally.

CHAPTER THIRTEEN

In which Mr. Joliffe makes a discovery

It was at this precise moment that Virginie saw the three of them together. Sophy was wearing the Hale diamonds. These had been purchased in Paris by his lordship's grandfather and were fashioned *en tremblant,* with the largest stones set on tiny coils so that they quivered and shimmered every time Sophy moved. The combination of Lysander's smile and the diamonds that she had so hoped would be hers turned Virginie's heart to stone. Turning to Bunny, she said with a brittle laugh, "Look at Hale smiling like that at your wife. I wonder how he dares, and with his own wife sitting right next to her!"

"What do you mean?" replied Bunny, dragging his eyes away from her décolletage. "Hale? Where? Why shouldn't he smile?"

"You mean you don't know?"

"Know? Know what? What is there to know?" Bunny's eyes were now turned to the Earl talking to Sally, who was looking up at him with an expression he found disturbing.

"Why, their affair. Surely you know that Hale and Sally were lovers? Years ago, of course! I thought everyone knew."

"Their *affair... lovers*?" cried Bunny in disbelief. "What in God's name are you talking about?"

"Hush!" said Virginie. "Everyone is looking! Don't make a scene!"

"I don't believe it! You are mistaken!" Bunny lowered his voice, but still spoke with vehemence. "They have never been more than passing acquaintances."

"I vow you will find I am not mistaken," replied Virginie silkily. "I will leave you to think about it." She patted his arm and, using her favorite trick, waved in the direction of a friend who was not really there, and left him.

In a daze, Bunny went back into the card room. Absentmindedly, he took and drank another glass of claret from a passing footman, and then another. He sat, thinking furiously back to the time after the birth of Ruth. He remembered that he had begun a liaison with a flirty little piece, what was her name? Julianna Something, he thought it was. For once, Sally had not turned reproachful eyes upon him. In fact, she had seemed downright happy. He recalled it all now. He had put it down to happiness at being a young mother, but in retrospect, it must have been something else, because only a few weeks later, she was a positive misery, weeping all the time. Enough to make you sick. Yes, now that he thought about it, it made perfect sense. A footman went by and he took another glass.

Conversing with Sally, Lord and Lady Hale had been joined by Lady Threlfall and the talk soon turned to subjects that women find fascinating and gentlemen do not. With a bow, and muttering something about a glass of wine, his lordship therefore took his leave and made his way to the card room. He had no sooner entered when he was accosted by Bunny Joliffe, who by now had convinced himself that what Virginie had said was quite right, and was drunk enough to speak without fear of the consequences.

"By God, Hale," he slurred, grabbing the other man by the arm, "I shall have satisfaction."

"What on earth is the matter, Joliffe?" replied the Earl. "Remove your hand from my arm. You're drunk."

This incensed the wronged husband even more. "Drunk?" he said in a voice loud with anger. "Me? Drunk? I've only had a couple of glasses of the piss-water they call wine in this house. I shall have satisfaction, I say. You and my wife? How dare you, sir! You will meet me. Name your Seconds!"

Conversation and card play had ceased all around. Everyone heard the accusation and the challenge. Lysander was stunned. But after moment's reflection, he knew it was useless to remonstrate. The man was drunk and angry beyond reason. Furthermore, he was in the right.

He pulled himself up to his full height, looked down at the other man and said, "Very well. Charles Alverstoke will act for me."

And he strode out of the room.

The echo of what was happening had just begun to be heard in the salon, when the Earl went up to his wife, and with the briefest of bows announced to her companions, "Forgive me. My wife is looking a trifle peaked. We shall be leaving now."

He took the astonished Sophy by the arm and propelled her towards the door, where their equally astonished hosts were afforded the same excuse and a polite but rapid farewell. Their cloaks were brought and in less than ten minutes they were in their carriage.

"Good heavens, Lysander!" cried Sophy once they were ensconced. "What can the matter be? What has happened?"

Her husband did not know where to start. He had to confess his affair with Sally Joliffe and announce that after all these years her husband had decided to seek satisfaction for it. He could hardly believe it himself, let alone explain it.

"If it's about Sally Joliffe," said Sophy earnestly as her husband hesitated, "I know all about it. Lady Threlfall told me and Sally confirmed it."

If Lysander was hesitant before, he was dumbstruck now. "What? Wh... when did you find this out?" he stammered.

"About a month ago. You know I took Lady Threlfall a watercolor and it... it came up in conversation"

"*It came up in conversation*? How in God's name does a thing like that come up in conversation?"

"Well," said Sophy reluctantly, "actually, I asked her."

"You *asked* her? After I specifically told you not to?"

He looked out of the carriage window, trying to control his anger. "Well, my dear," he said in a hard, cold voice, "let me be the first to inform you that not only do you now know, but Bunny Joliffe has also learned the truth. I find it difficult to believe this is just a coincidence. Your actions have somehow led to the fact that he is demanding satisfaction. He has called me out. I hope that if one or the other of us is seriously injured you will think it was worthwhile satisfying your idle curiosity."

It was Sophy's turn to be dumbfounded, and then both terrified and wildly angry. "A duel?" she cried. "It cannot be! They are not permitted anymore! He cannot! You cannot!"

"Oh yes he can, and I must. I am honor bound to meet him at a time and place of his choosing, though I may choose the weapon. Goddam it, Sophy, do you see what you have done?"

"But I didn't mean…! You can't! He can't! It's impossible!" cried Sophy desperately, but her husband turned his face away and said nothing.

They sat apart the rest of the way home. Lysander's outward demeanor betrayed nothing, but Sophy could not stop trembling. Fear and rage warred in her breast. At last they arrived at Hale House.

Then Lysander said calmly and firmly. "I am going to see Charles. He will act for me. You are to go up to bed in a perfectly normal way. You will not speak or give anyone the idea that anything is amiss. I will be back as soon as I can and we will talk then."

He handed her down from the carriage and gave the order to be driven on.

It took every ounce of her willpower for Sophy to walk in the front door and return Pennyworth's greeting in an even tone, telling him that his lordship had gone to see Charles Alverstoke on a matter of business. She slowly mounted the stairs and went first to the nursery. She kissed her sleeping child's curly head and stood for a moment, wondering if he might one day be in the same situation as his father, facing a duel over an affair of honor. Honor! How she despised the very concept that could make a man jeopardize his life and thus his family's welfare over something so trivial. Then she went slowly to her bedchamber where Susan was waiting for her.

She was still in her evening gown and diamonds, with an elaborate coiffure. If Susan thought her ladyship's almost total silence odd, she said nothing, but simply removed the myriad pins from her hair, brushed out her curls and put the Hale diamonds into their velvet boxes. As she undressed and put on her nightgown, Sophy wondered how Bunny Joliffe had discovered the truth about his wife and Lysander. The only people she had spoken to were Clara Threlfall and Sally herself, but Clara was a well-known gossip and could easily have reported her conversation. But to whom? Who would be interested in that old history?

Remembering the many glances of barely disguised dislike that Virginie Beaufort had given her over the years, Sophy was suddenly sure that she was involved. Everyone knew she was Bunny's latest mistress, and she was the only one who stood to benefit by creating the scandal. Yes, it had to be her!

But knowing how the problem had arisen went nowhere in solving it. Sophy resolved to go and see Sally the next day. She was sure Sally would be as anxious as she to find a solution. It was impossible for this duel to go ahead. It was medieval! Something would have to be done. She scribbled a note to Sally Joliffe, and asked Susan to hand it to Pennyworth for delivery that night, immediately, in spite of the late hour.

When her husband returned, she was quite calm. He led her into his bedchamber and pulled out a chair next to his desk.

"Normally one does not talk about these things with women," he said, looking at her seriously, "but I think it better that you know so as to save you the worry of uncertainty."

He hesitated a moment, then continued. "Charles will call on Joliffe tomorrow and find out who his Seconds are to be. They will together decide the day and place. It will be pistols, of course. It's a pity swords are no longer in use because I would have been able to simply pink him and it would all be over. Pistols are a far different affair. I shall delope in any case. Fire in the air. It's the only honorable thing to do. I am to blame, after all."

Sophy could hardly believe what she was hearing. "Oh! Men and their honor!" she burst out. "You might be killed! Can't Charles do anything about it? It's all so stupid!" She had to fight not to panic.

"Charles will do what is right, you may be sure of that. His first responsibility is to try to find a way to avoid the duel, though I don't imagine Joliffe will accommodate him. He's always been pigheaded and his honor is at stake. I don't suppose you will ever understand how important honor is to a gentleman." He was silent for a moment. "Try not to worry, my love. We Hales can face anything, after all, you know it's the family motto: *Potentia et Honor*: Might and Honor. I've never heard that Joliffe was anything of a shot." He attempted a small laugh. "Come on, let's go to bed."

But she couldn't. She strode around the room, tears falling unchecked down her cheeks. "It's all my fault!" she cried. "I had no idea... if only I'd known!" Then she turned to her husband, clutching at a straw of hope. "You said Charles would try to find a way for the duel not to take place. How could that be achieved?"

"Joliffe would have to be prepared to accept some other satisfaction. Since he did not strike me, he could just demand a public apology. If he had struck me, a duel would be the only way to settle it. There are rules."

"What rules? Who decided all this?"

"There is a Code. The *Code Duello*. A gentleman learns this when he is quite young."

"So, Bunny could be satisfied with an apology? But would you apologize? You didn't really do anything wrong!" Sophy was desperate.

"Sophy! I had an affair with the man's wife!"

"Yes, but he didn't care! And he has had affairs with many women!"

"He would have cared if he had known about it. Not because he loved Sally, but for his honor, I'm sure of that. And whether he had his own infidelities has nothing to do with it. But in answer to your question, no, I would not like to have to give a public apology. A duel is private and, because very few people witness it, quickly forgotten. A public apology would be remembered forever. It would be a mark on the family name. In any case, I'm sure Joliffe will never agree to it, I wouldn't, in his position."

"But Lysander!" she cried hysterically. "What if he kills you?"

He went to her and drew her into his arms. "As I said, I've never heard that Joliffe is a good shot, and it's hard to hit someone at any distance. You must calm down and try to get some sleep, for both our sakes."

Sophy allowed herself to be led back to bed, but she lay sleepless most of the night, with one idea churning in her brain. *He must be allowed to apologize. He must. He must.*

CHAPTER FOURTEEN

In which her ladyship seeks help

The following morning a hollow-eyed Sophy went into the nursery, trying to appear more cheerful than she felt. Sylvester was overjoyed when she said he was to have breakfast with his Papa. She couldn't shake off the idea that the boy might lose his father. Every minute he could spend with him was precious.

Thrilled to be able to have something other than his customary porridge, the boy sat there stuffing buttered muffins into his mouth as fast as he could.

"A gentleman does not reach for a second muffin while he still has the last one in his mouth," reprimanded the stern Papa. "Put it back."

"But Papa! I very yike muffins," said his son, nevertheless reluctantly replacing the muffin.

"You will ask Mama politely if you may have another of her muffins."

"Mama, I peese have 'nother muffin, peese?" said Sylvester appealingly. But Sophy had just received a note from Sally Joliffe and was preoccupied. Receiving no answer, he repeated, "'Nother muffin, peese, Mama?"

"Sorry, my darling, what did you say?" answered Sophy, finally realizing her son's eyes were fixed upon her.

"Your son, my love, is very politely asking if he may have another of your muffins," said Lysander, wondering what had her attention so completely.

"Of course, darling! You may have as many muffins as you like!" she replied, whereupon Sylvester grabbed three from the plate all at once, and his father sighed.

"You will never be fit for company with so indulgent a Mama!" he said. Picking up his newspaper, he continued to his wife, "You are so absorbed with your note, I presume I may read the paper. I can only suppose it is a *billet doux* from an admirer." His tone showed her he was determined to act naturally in spite of the sword hanging over their heads.

"Yes! That's exactly what it is!" said Sophy, following his lead. She gave a little laugh, belying the panic she felt in the pit of her stomach. "It's from an admirer who has the peculiarity of being attracted to a married matron with a butter-faced child!"

"I can't blame him, I have the same peculiarity," said her husband looking at her over the top of his newspaper, and giving her his bewitching smile. She had to blink back her tears. Luckily, Sylvester was so involved in licking butter from his fingers, he didn't notice, and Lysander understood. But she did not tell him the contents of the note, and his breeding prevented him from asking.

After breakfast her ladyship called for her carriage, telling her husband she had a couple of things she wished to purchase at the Pantheon Bazaar. This was a delightful conglomeration of businesses between Tyburn Road and Marlborough Street, where one could buy anything from stockings to stovepipes. It was one of her favorite haunts and she often bought gifts there to send to the housekeeper and her son who still lived with her father in the village of her birth.

Today, nothing appealed to her less than such an outing. In fact, she was going to the Joliffes' residence. Sally had begged her to come over that morning. Sophy had her driver put her down a little way away from their front door, since she did not want her very recognizable carriage to be seen there. Sally was watching for her and came herself to the door as soon as she saw her approach the front of the house.

"Come upstairs to my apartments," she said in her pleasant, low voice. Bunny will certainly not see us there."

She was led into a spacious, bright room overlooking the garden at the back of the house. It was decorated in shades of turquoise green, now very faded and rather shabby.

"This color did not wear well, I'm afraid," said Sally, as she saw Sophy looking about her. "I chose it when I was first married and had little experience of these things. My aunt said it would fade, but, of course, I thought I knew it all! But, please do sit down."

Sophy sat, thinking how long it must have been since the room was refurbished, compared with her own, which Lysander was constantly urging her to update. How patiently Sally endured such neglect! What she did not know was that her friend could have spent her own money on renovations, but did not, as she had always been conscious of the difference between her own wealth and that of her husband. She had never wanted to make this difference felt. Even after all she had endured, in her heart of hearts, she still loved him.

Her visitor came right to the point. "Sally," she said firmly, "I asked you to receive me because I am hoping that between us we can somehow put an end to this dreadful duel. Lysander says it will be pistols and he's going to delope, fire in the air, you know. Bunny may kill him, and if he does, he'll have to leave the country. So we would both lose our husbands over this silly affair! I am so sick of hearing about the *honor of a gentleman*. There must be something we can do!"

She hesitated a minute, then continued, "Lysander tells me that according to the rules of the *Code Duello*, which, apparently they all learn while still at their mother's breast, the wronged party may, if he has not actually struck the person he challenged, accept an apology. Lysander doesn't want to do that. He says a duel would be more quickly forgotten, whatever the outcome. Anyway, he says that as a matter of honor, Bunny will never propose it. But if Bunny sends his Seconds with the offer of accepting an apology instead of a duel, I don't see how, *in honor*, Lysander can refuse it."

She paused, then went on. "Sally, do you think you can induce Bunny to put aside this honor nonsense and direct his Seconds to say he'll accept an apology? Could you perhaps persuade your husband by a great flood of tears, saying it will kill you if he is wounded, or has to leave the country or something like that?"

"Alas," said Sally, sadly. "I'm not sure the threat of my death would persuade him. I'm the one with the bulk of the fortune, you know. It would give him both money and the freedom to lavish it on Virginie Beaufort. He would probably be all the happier."

"So you think Virginie had something to do with this?"

"Yes, I don't know how she did, but I'd stake anything on it."

"I feel the same, Sally! We can't let her win!"

"No we can't," agreed Sally slowly. "Wait a minute...!" She thought for a moment and her face cleared. "Ye...es, there may be something I can do. Leave it with me."

"I will. Thank you, Sally," said Sophy, standing up, "I think it best if I not linger. Lysander would be furious if he knew I was here and I can't imagine Bunny would be pleased either."

They went quietly downstairs and, after exchanging a warm embrace, the ladies parted. The whole visit had not lasted much more than half an hour. Sophy walked quickly to her waiting carriage and told the driver to make for the Pantheon Bazaar. She had no desire to go there but even less did she want to tell a total lie to her husband. So she wandered around, not really seeing anything, in the end purchasing a length of ribbon that matched nothing in her wardrobe, and a bunch of silk flowers that, once she got them home, she decided were hideous.

Meanwhile, Sally returned thoughtfully upstairs and composed a note to the Vyse family solicitor, asking him to wait on her at his earliest convenience. The solicitor who had handled her marriage settlements had since been succeeded by his son. Luckily, this gentleman enjoyed society and was well informed about the latest *on-dits*. The same could not have been said of his father, who held himself above the dealings of the world, considering his advice better if detached from everyday affairs. It was Ernest Grimes the Younger who therefore waited on Sally Joliffe shortly after luncheon. He was a spare man of middle age, dressed very soberly and wearing a pince-nez.

"Mr. Grimes," began Sally in her low, musical voice, once she had invited him to be seated, "I am sorry to be so frank, and to come to the point so abruptly, but I believe time is of the essence. You may be aware that my husband has involved himself in an... unfortunate disagreement with Lord Hale and has called him out."

The solicitor nodded. "Yes, Madam, I have heard the news. Most regrettable."

"I am anxious that this duel be avoided, as I fear... I fear my husband may be injured. I'm sure Lord Hale is a better shot than he."

Mr. Grimes nodded again. "Yes," he agreed. "I have heard him described as such."

"I therefore wish to know what... financial inducements, or even, though I hesitate to use the word, threats that I could make that would discourage him from continuing. Is there, perhaps, something that can be done in respect of the settlements made upon my husband at the time of our marriage?"

The solicitor's eyebrows rose, and a faint smile creased his cheeks. "Hmm... let me see..." He took a heavy brown folder from the large leather satchel he had brought with him. It had the legend *Vyse Family* written on the cover in an old-fashioned gold script. He turned over three quarters of the pages until he came to a sheet that apparently provided the information he required. He studied it carefully then lifted his head and said, "There is a clause that will, I believe, help you."

He read, "*Whereas, if either the party of the first part, hereinafter Sarah Mariah Joliffe née Vyse, or the party of the second part, hereinafter Beauchamp Redcliffe Joliffe, should find incontrovertible evidence that the union of Sarah Mariah Joliffe nee Vyse and Beauchamp Redcliffe Joliffe is rendered unsustainable, unwarranted, untenable, ill-founded or flawed by such issues such as, but not limited to, non-consummation, illegal, adulterous, cruel or abnormal action or physical or mental defect on the part of either of the aforementioned parties, the union may be deemed to be terminated, whether or not divorce may be obtained in law, and the settlements laid out in paragraphs I-IV of this document be rendered null and void.*"

He put the paper down and adjusted his pince-nez. "In other words, dear lady, you may, for the reasons outlined above, namely, in brief, an illegal, adulterous, cruel or abnormal action on your husband's part, setting aside physical or mental defect, apply to have the settlements rendered null and void." He paused a moment, then continued, "Dueling is, of course, illegal and that in itself may be enough for the dissolution of the agreement." He looked directly at her. "And, if I may mention it without causing you distress, Mr. Joliffe's current… er… liaison with Mrs. Virginie Beauchamp, which I believe no one to be ignorant of, is of course adulterous. It would not be hard, I imagine, to find a witness or witnesses who could testify as to having seen Mr. Joliffe enter her premises on a number of occasions and not leave till several hours later. It is also possible that a person in her employ could be encouraged to testify, should that be required."

He removed his pince-nez and polished the lenses before looking up at her again, to say, with complete disregard of what his esteemed parent would have said in the same situation, "I could myself help you in that matter, if necessary."

For Mr. Grimes was not a supporter of Bunny Joliffe. He had followed his amorous adventures for some years, wondering why a gentleman married to such an attractive and gentle wife as Sally should find it necessary to stray from his own hearth.

It would have surprised and gratified Sally to know that her lawyer held her so close to his heart, but she was still thinking about what he had read out. "My goodness!" she said wonderingly, "all these years I never knew that such a clause existed. You know, I was never involved in the marriage settlements. I was simply told they had been made. Your father handled them, I believe." She received a confirmatory nod. "How far-sighted he must have been to put in that clause, and how odd of Bunny not to have noticed it."

"My father acted his whole life as solicitor for your family, dear Mrs. Joliffe, and he would have wanted to ensure your wellbeing. As I do myself," and though he was seated, he bowed. "And I believe Mr. Joliffe may have signed the papers without reading them through. His... er, haste to marry you may, I fear, have affected his judgement. Now, perhaps it would be useful if I were to jot down the relevant words from this clause."

He withdrew from his black leather satchel a half-quarto sheet of paper (no need to waste such a precious commodity), a pen and a bottle of ink. He unscrewed the top from the ink, placed the bottle on an adjacent small table, fitted a nib into the pen and carefully wrote out four or five lines. From his seemingly bottomless satchel he then drew a powder box from which he shook a fine sand to dry the ink.

"You have certainly come prepared, Mr. Grimes!" marveled Sally. "I do not know how to thank you. It is such a relief to know that one's affairs are in the hands of such competent advisors. What you have told me will most certainly be useful. Let us leave for the moment the question of witnesses to my husband's... infidelity, but I will surely contact you again, should it be necessary. Now, please will you take a glass of sherry before you go?"

"That would be most welcome, I thank you," replied the solicitor.

CHAPTER FIFTEEN

In which Mr. Joliffe is surprised

Mr. Grimes and his client then spent a cozy fifteen minutes discussing family matters, the progress of the Joliffe daughters and, somewhat to Sally's surprise, the education of his own twin sons. They were in the middle of this discussion when Bunny Joliffe arrived home.

He had spent the afternoon with Virginie who had tried, with limited success, to bolster his courage for the duel. He knew he was a poor shot at best, and thought Lord Hale would be a formidable opponent. That morning he had already begun to regret issuing the challenge. He had awoken with a dreadful headache and the certainty he had done something very stupid while in his cups. It was not helped when he went to his club and was met by almost universal shaken heads and commiseration.

All Virginie could say to soothe him was that it might not be too bad. She didn't think Lysander would try to kill him. She also broached the subject of his leaving his wife. He knew she had been unfaithful once, and in all likelihood, more than once. Bunny's mind was in such turmoil by this time that he hardly knew what to do. He finally decided, very unusually for him, to come home in the middle of the afternoon. He was now surprised to see his wife sitting drinking sherry amicably with a man he felt he should recognize but did not. Mr. Grimes rose when he came in, and having shaken his client's husband by the hand with discernable lack of enthusiasm, took his leave.

"What's that feller bin doin' here?" he grumbled to his wife. "Not another of your lovers!"

"Don't be ridiculous, Bunny," responded Sally, with a distinctly sharp tone in her usually musical voice. "I do not have lovers. I had a brief affair with Lysander Barrington years ago, which I would not have done if you had been a better husband. You are as much to blame as I, or more, since your infidelities were even then the talk of the town. For you to have challenged Lord Hale is the purest folly."

Bunny was astonished to hear his wife speak to him in this tone. She had always had a low, soothing voice. Even at her most upset, she had never before spoken to him sharply.

"What was I supposed to do? Seein' him smiling at you like that and then hearing from Vir… from someone that you had been his mistress."

"I see, so all of this is because Virginie Beaufort pointed out Lord Hale smiling at me *and at his wife* and then telling you I had been involved with him years ago? Bunny, did it ever occur to you to wonder *why* she was telling you this? Do not you think she had some ulterior motive? Anyway, please sit down. There is something I wish to say to you." She gestured towards a chair opposite her.

Bunny Joliffe sat down, feeling that the world he knew had somehow disappeared and he was now in a strange universe.

"I asked Mr. Grimes to come here because I wanted to know about the settlements made on you when we were married," continued his wife in a voice quite unlike her own. "It was most instructive. He informed me that in the event of either of us committing an action," and she read from the sheet of paper the solicitor had given her, emphasizing certain words, "*such as, but not limited to, **illegal**, **adulterous**, cruel or abnormal... the union may be deemed to be terminated, whether or not divorce may be obtained in law, and the **settlements** laid out in paragraphs I-IV of this document be **rendered null and void**.* In other words, Bunny, since dueling is illegal, if you engage in a duel, I may claim that our union is at an end and the settlements will no longer be forthcoming. In addition, given the fact that you have also committed adultery many times over, for which Mr. Grimes assures me evidence may easily be obtained, no court would hesitate in terminating our agreement. Of course, you may also claim that my adultery is cause to terminate our union, but in either case, the settlements will be made null and void. It matters not to me as I received nothing in the settlements. The money is mine and it will revert to me."

Bunny was speechless. It had never occurred to him that the support he received from the Vyse family could be withdrawn. Mr. Grimes was correct when he said that he had never read the contract. He had been only too eager to sign it, a fact of which Mr. Grimes the Elder had taken advantage. Coming as it did after a day of increasing regret at having issued the challenge in the first place, this news put the final nail in the coffin of his pretentions.

"But what the hell am I supposed to do?" he spluttered. "I've already issued the challenge, God help me. I'll be lucky if Hale doesn't kill me."

"Hale is a gentleman. He will not try to kill you, but in any duel the unexpected may happen and someone may be seriously hurt. I refuse to allow that to happen in my name to either you or Lysander. Therefore, if you continue with this challenge, I will leave you and take my daughters and my fortune with me."

"But I cannot withdraw now!" cried her husband. "I'll be labelled a coward and my life in London will be over. Sally, my dear, you must see reason!"

It was many years since her husband had addressed her as *my dear* except with the utmost irony, and the words were soft on her ear, but Sally held firm. "You are to tell your Seconds that you are prepared to accept a public apology. I understand that this is acceptable where the challenger has not struck his opponent. Let us hope that Hale may be persuaded to do that. It is your only hope, Bunny."

With that, Sally rose to her feet and swept out of the room.

Later that evening Lord and Lady Hale were in the family sitting room playing a game of piquet, on which neither was really concentrating, when the front door knocker sounded and Charles Alverstoke was shown into the room.

"Charles!" cried her ladyship, gladly abandoning her cards and standing to greet him.

"Damned glad to see you!" said his lordship, packing up the cards. He strode over and shook his friend warmly by the hand.

"I've got some... er... news about, well, about... you know," said Charles, hesitating, looking between Lysander and Sophy.

"If you mean the duel," said Sophy, "you may as well talk in front of me, as I know all about it."

Lysander shrugged and nodded his consent, and Charles dropped down into one of the armchairs. "The most extraordinary thing," he said. "Had a visit from Monty Burnham, Bunny's Second, y'know." They both nodded. "Says Bunny's ready to accept a public apology. Doesn't want to challenge you, Sandy. Don't blame him, mark you. He was looking queer as Dick's hatband when I saw him in the club earlier today. But it's damned odd!"

"Oh, thank goodness! She did it!" cried Sophy.

Both men stared at her.

"Well, when we talked about it last night, Lysander, you said that an apology was a possibility when one person had not struck the other. The Code, you said, didn't you?"

"I did, though I distinctly remember saying I abhorred the idea," said her husband slowly. "But what I do not understand is how Joliffe arrived at the notion. I would have bet anything against it."

He looked hard at his wife, who was staring at her hands in her lap. "Sophy, look at me!" She raised her head. "What have you done?" His tone was harsh.

Sophy hesitated, then lifted her chin and said defiantly, "I went to see Sally Joliffe. She agreed with me that all this honor stuff may be important for men, but we women prefer to arrange things differently. She was going to talk to Bunny and persuade him to accept an apology. Evidently, she has done so. You need not worry, in no way did it appear that the request had come from you. In fact, I told her you didn't like the idea."

"Charles, I'm going to have to ask you to leave," said his lordship, his lips now white with anger, "I need to talk to my wife. Pennyworth will see you out."

"Come on, Sandy. She acted for the best," replied Charles recognizing the look on his friend's face. "No need for a tiff, don't y' know."

"When I need your advice on talking to my wife, Charles," said his lordship in a voice colder than he had ever used with him before, "I shall ask for it."

Charles bit his lip, shook his head, kissed Sophy's hand, and left.

"But you shouldn't be vexed with me, Lysander!" cried Sophy when they were alone. "This is a much better outcome. After all, you said yourself that you are guilty of an affair with his wife. And if he had killed you, he would have had to leave the country. Both Sally and I would have been left alone with our children. An apology is better than that!"

"God dammit, Sophy," cried the Earl in a rage. "I am so tired of your interfering! Why won't you leave well enough alone? I would have deloped, he would have missed, and it would all have been over and forgotten in a matter of days. Now I shall have to grovel in public, rake up Sally's name and generally make a fool of myself and the House of Hale! This will be the talk of the clubs for years to come. Good God, even Sylvester may hear about it!"

"So, it's your pride again! You would prefer to die than to admit you did something wrong! Well, I won't let you! Anything could happen in a duel! You could slip while deloping and hit him, or he could have unexpected luck and hit you! Either one of you could get killed and it's *illegal*, Lysander, *illegal*! You might die, and if you killed him, you would have to leave the country! In either case, what would become of Sylvester and me? Your pride is not only misplaced, it's selfish! I cannot believe you would actually prefer to fight him! It's just plain nonsense!"

"You will never understand the importance of a man's honor, Sophy, and I am not going to waste my time trying to explain it any more. But I am very, very displeased with you!"

"And I am very, very displeased with you! Don't you dare try to teach this rubbish to Sylvester, I shall not allow it!"

"My son will be a gentleman with a gentleman's honor, and nothing you can say or do will change that. These are things entirely outside your responsibility as his mother. Please don't say another word, Sophy. I really cannot discuss it any longer. Go to bed."

"That is the only sensible thing you've said so far!" retorted Sophy. "I hope not to see you again until you've come to your senses!" and, like Sally Joliffe some hours before, swept out of the room.

His lordship waited a moment, strode to the door and shouted, "Brandy, at once!"

When Pennyworth silently came in with a bottle and a glass, he gestured towards a table. The butler put down his tray and left without a word, quietly closing the door. For only the third time in his life, and the other two occasions had also been caused by disagreements with his wife, the Earl steadily consumed a whole bottle of brandy. He had to be helped to his bed at three in the morning by Pennyworth and Winton.

CHAPTER SIXTEEN

In which Lord Hale loses his temper

The following morning, with a head that felt as if it were in a vice and a tongue like sandpaper, his lordship took himself off to Gentleman Jackson's boxing salon and put himself and several sparring partners through a punishing ordeal, until the Champion himself called a halt.

"No good trying to draw the cork of everyone in the place, me lud," he said. "I hears as how you've got problems with some gobble-cock, but you won't solve it by drawing a lot of claret here. Go home!"

Having been hosed down liberally by the freezing water provided for the refreshment of clients at the boxing salon and his headache now effectively purged, the Earl did as he was advised.

Her ladyship, whom he had not laid eyes on since their altercation the previous night, was still not to be seen, so he ate a solitary luncheon of a large helping of roast beef and mustard. Though this went some way to improving his physical condition, it did nothing for his state of mind. He wandered up to the nursery to see if playing with his young son could relieve the anger and frustration he felt at the prospect of the impending Apology. He was foiled in this, however. Neither his son nor Daisy was there. Pennyworth informed him her ladyship had gone back to the Pantheon Bazaar, taking Daisy and Sylvester with her.

She had noticed on her trip there the previous day that one of the enterprises had quite a menagerie of animals, which she thought would interest his young lordship. They did indeed, especially the monkeys, which was not surprising as, according to his mother, he was one himself.

Muttering furious imprecations that his whole family had deserted him, his lordship went into his study and tried to relieve his mind by reading his old friend Marcus Aurelius. He knew that the philosopher's chief advice was always to calmly accept the inevitable and not waste time struggling against it. It was counsel that in his present frame of mind, he found hard to read and even harder to implement.

So when, an hour or so later, Charles arrived at Hale House with the intelligence that Joliffe's Seconds had chosen ten o'clock that evening at Brooke's for the Apology, his anger and frustration had by no means abated. The time was well chosen from Joliffe's point of view. Most members would have dined by then and the place would be full. His lips set in a straight line, his lordship agreed curtly but refused to engage in any discussion with his friend. Charles said he would meet him there, and left, shaking his head.

Shortly after Charles' departure, her ladyship returned home with their son, who ran into the house shouting, "Papa! Papa! I seed the monkeys! They was so funny! They went like this." He gibbered and capered all around the hall exactly like the monkeys he had seen, much to the amusement of the footmen, until his father, in a towering rage that had nothing to do with Sylvester or the monkeys, came out of his study.

"Sylvester!" he thundered, "Cease this din immediately! What do you imagine this is? A public marketplace? Go to the nursery at once!"

There was immediate silence. The footmen straightened up and the smiles faded from their lips. Sylvester took one stricken look at his father, his god, the center of his existence, and burst into tears. He ran to hide behind his mother's skirts. Sophy, lifting her chin, her eyes blazing fury at her husband, picked up her son and walked immediately upstairs with him sobbing in her arms. His lordship hesitated for a moment, then went back into his study, closing the door with a deliberate and ominously gentle click.

Inside his study, he stood stock still as the realization of what he had done dawned upon him. He knew his son loved him above all things, and the vision of Sylvester's shocked little face when he had thundered at him for no reason burned before his eyes. He groaned and fell into his chair, putting his head in his hands. He stayed like that for some time, reflecting with horror that he, Lysander Barrington, fifth Earl of Hale, head of one of the great families of England, educated at Eton and Oxford, owner of a library of classical philosophy that he read, as he believed, for its power to edify, was no better than an illiterate lout with no control over his temper. At last, he slowly stood up, left the room and went upstairs, to make his first apology of the day.

In the nursery, Sophy had succeeded in calming the wild sobbing of her son, and had sent Daisy to the kitchen to find cakes, or muffins or trifle, or anything that he particularly liked, to help compensate for his unhappiness. For the little boy was genuinely sad.

"Why Papa vexed with me, Mama? I not bin a good boy?" he asked pitifully, lifting his wretched little face to hers as he began to cry again.

"You are a very good boy," said his mother soothingly. "Papa loves you very much and he doesn't mean to shout at you." For even in her anger with her husband, Sophy knew this was true. "He isn't vexed with you. Something else is troubling him."

"What troublin' him?"

"He has to do something he doesn't want to do, and he's afraid men will laugh at him."

"I 'tect him, Mama! I kill those mens with my sword!"

At that point, his lordship came into the nursery.

"Here is your Papa now," said Sophy. "You tell him that." She handed Sylvester to her husband without speaking to or looking at him, and left them alone.

As she walked towards her own bedchamber, she saw Daisy returning with a covered tray.

"Don't go in there yet," she said. "Sylvester is with his father. Let them talk."

In the nursery, Lysander had taken his son on his knee and kissed the top of his curly head.

"I'm sorry I was so angry with you, my son," he said. "I should not have shouted at you. You did nothing wrong. In any case, a gentleman does not shout at those smaller and weaker than himself. I did not act like a gentleman. Please forgive me."

"I f'give you, Papa," said the little man, looking up at his father. "Mama says mens troubin you. I 'tect you. I kill them with my sword."

"That's just the point," Lysander gave a little laugh. "We're not allowed to kill them with our sword. We have to say we're sorry. That's much harder than using a sword. But thank you. I'm much happier knowing that you would protect me. Now, tell me about those monkeys."

Thus encouraged, Sylvester regaled his father with a description and demonstration of the monkeys, so that quite soon he was capering around the room and they were both laughing. Hearing them, Daisy brought in the boy's supper tray, which had on it, joy of joys, a helping of trifle.

"Cook thought you wouldn't mind the young master 'avin an 'elping of your trifle, me lord," she said, "seein' as 'ow 'e was so sad."

"Of course, he deserves it much more than I."

Father and son sat together and chatted as Sylvester ate his supper, and then his lordship took them both down to the kitchen for more trifle.

"Another small serving for my son and a large serving for me," he announced to Mrs. Green.

"Before your dinner, me lord?" asked the cook, scandalized.

"Yes. Today I shall have trifle before dinner. In fact, I shall have trifle *for* dinner, so make it a very large helping."

"But Papa, you dint eat your vegebles," protested the young master.

"So I didn't. Very well, I shall have a plate of vegetables and a helping of trifle."

This was duly served, and his lordship, who, like his son, genuinely disliked vegetables, was forced to eat a plate of peas and carrots before his dessert. A very lenient punishment, he reflected, for his behavior.

Lysander said he would give his son his bath and put him to bed, which he did, with a great deal more splashing and disarray than was usually warranted by the exercise. It was necessary to demonstrate once more the floating qualities of wood, using the toy boats Sylvester had in his bath. Even when the boats were subjected to missiles from above, in the shape of a duck, which the Earl claimed had been shot out of the sky by Uncle Charles, who, as everyone knew, was a very good shot, and which fell upon them with a great splash, the boats still did not sink. Naturally, this had to be demonstrated several times, for the sake of science. Both man and boy were oblivious to the resulting pool of water on the nursery floor, Sylvester because he did not see it, and Lysander because he had never been required to clean up a mess in his life. The Earl put his son to bed and told him a story, in this case, about the wooden horse of Troy, and Sylvester fell asleep to dream of being transported inside a horse, climbing out of a trapdoor and attacking everything in sight with his wooden sword.

Now that he was in a calmer state of mind, his lordship still hesitated before going down to his study to consider exactly how he would frame the Apology. He was still angry with his wife for putting him in this situation, and her silent blaze of fury at his treatment of Sylvester told him he was far from being forgiven himself. It was best not to provoke another argument, he decided, and left her alone.

He called for a brandy. "Only one," he said to Pennyworth when it arrived. "Under no circumstances bring me more."

"Very well, my lord" answered the butler impassively, thinking, nonetheless, how he would ever be able to avoid his lordship having more, short of hiding all the bottles in the house, an impossible task considering there were several hundred in the cellar.

An hour or so later, his lordship went up to his bedchamber and, summoning Winton, arrayed himself in his finest formal evening clothes. Over black trousers and shoes, he wore a long tailed dark grey superfine coat, cut so perfectly that it seemed molded to his body, without being the remotest bit tight anywhere. He needed no buckram to fill out his shoulders and his narrow waist and hips required no excessive seaming of his coat to provide the latest nipped-in waist shape of gentlemen's attire. The coat was cut away in the front to reveal a white waistcoat and neckcloth, folded tonight with special care. He wore no jewelry except a gold watch with a heavy gold chain across his waistcoat, on his right-hand middle finger the Hale family signet ring with the script H on the face, and on the fourth finger of his left hand, the wide old gold ring that Sophy had given him on their first Christmas and which he never removed.

Winton sighed with pleasure when the Earl was ready. A valet was judged by the appearance of his master, and Winton knew that in this he had no peer. His lordship, tall, with broad shoulders and a slim though muscular physique, was a valet's dream. He might have wished, on occasion, that his master be more adventurous in the matter of waistcoats and jewelry. He never carried a snuff box, for example, and refused even the most unobtrusive fob on his heavy watch chain, and he always wore the most sober of waistcoats. But in all other respects Winton found his appearance perfect.

When the Earl strode into Brooke's shortly before ten o'clock, no one without prior knowledge would have guessed that he was there to perform a task he found demeaning and exceedingly disagreeable. He held himself erect but appeared perfectly relaxed, and if he did not smile, neither was his brow creased with a frown. He was soon met by Charles Alverstoke, who had also donned evening attire, his black armband and waistcoat only adding to the formality of his appearance. They entered the main salon of the club. It was filled to capacity. Instinctively, a space was made for them in the center where they stood, side by side, until Monty Burnham appeared with Bunny Joliffe in his wake. The crowd waited in a foot-shifting silence until the last stroke of ten sounded on the grandfather clock in the corner of the salon.

Then Monty pronounced, "On behalf of Bunny... er... Beauchamp Joliffe, I ask whether Lord Hale is prepared to offer an apology for the wrong he has done Bunny... er, Mr. Joliffe."

Charles, at his most formal, answered, "On behalf of Lysander Barrington, Earl of Hale, I, Charles Alverstoke, answer in the affirmative. His lordship is prepared to offer an apology on the understanding that this satisfies the challenge issued to him by Mr. Joliffe."

After a muttered exchange between Bunny and Monty, the latter replied, "It is understood that the apology satisfies the challenge, yes."

The Seconds stood back and the Principles faced each other. Lysander drew himself to his full height, which was several inches taller than Bunny. Magnificent in physique and demeanor, there was nothing remotely ridiculous about him. There was not a sound in the room.

"Mr. Joliffe," began his lordship in a clear voice, "I sincerely regret that an indiscretion on my part some ten years ago has caused you pain. I am especially sorry that it may have brought shame upon your wife, who was then and still is, one of the loveliest and best women of my acquaintance. Save my own wife, there is no woman I admire more. I have no excuse to offer other than that I was young and your wife the most beautiful woman in London. You are a lucky man, Joliffe. No blame attaches to her for our liaison since, in my youthful ardor, I was relentless in my pursuit of her." He hesitated, then continued, "I hope we may shake hands and for the sake of both our families put this behind us."

The Earl advanced towards Bunny Joliffe with his hand outstretched. There was a collective sigh as a multitude of held breaths were expelled and the two men shook hands. Each of the Principals shook hands with the other's Seconds and then Charles and Monty shook hands with each other. His lordship gave a brief bow, Charles took his arm and they swiftly left the room and the club. Only by the tension Charles could feel in the muscles of his friend's upper arm could he perceive the emotion that Lysander was so effectively concealing. Once outside, he offered to go back with him to Hale House, or to take him to his own house. But his friend, not trusting himself to say much, replied curtly, "Thank you, Charles, but I prefer to walk home alone."

Back in the club, a gabble had broken out. Amongst those who remarked excitedly, "He pursued her!", "The most beautiful woman in London!", "Still admires her!" were the more thoughtful who agreed that it had been very well done. Hale had apologized with dignity and had protected the name of the lady, taking all the blame upon himself. In a strange way, he had flattered Bunny for being married to a woman who had held such attraction for him, when he could have had almost any woman in London.

Bunny certainly felt this himself and when, after a few glasses of claret, he left the club, it was not to Mount Street and Virginie that he bent his steps, but to his own home. Going into his wife's bedchamber for the first time in some years, he found her in bed. She knew what was happening at the Club, and was trying to interest herself in the latest edition of the *Mode Illustrée* from Paris. She was trying to decide whether the new wide sleeves would become her, but her attention had been constantly distracted as she anxiously wondered how the Apology had gone. Who she could obtain information from on the morrow? She did not expect her husband home at all, and was surprised, even shocked, to see him.

"Bunny!" she exclaimed. "What are you doing here... I mean, why are you home and... here? Is it over? Did Lord Hale apologize?"

"Yes, my dear," he replied, looking at her properly for the first time in years and seeing how pretty she was, especially in her nightgown with her hair tumbling from a very becoming lace cap. "It is over, and he made a handsome apology. Said you were the best-looking woman in London and he still admires you. If you hadn't married me, you might have had him, you know." For some reason, the realization of this pleased Bunny no end.

"But I loved you to distraction," replied his wife with a sigh. "I never looked at anyone else!"

"Do you still love me, a little?" murmured her husband, moving his hands towards the ribbons at the top of her nightgown.

"Of course I do," said Sally, coloring, as her husband's fingers moved beneath the cotton of her gown. "I have always loved you, even when... you didn't love me."

Bunny muttered something indistinct and put his lips to hers. Sally could not imagine what had happened to her husband, but because she did truly love him, she surrendered to his embrace and they made love for the first time in years. The irony is that Virginie had managed to teach him a little finesse and his performance was the best it had ever been. They were both breathless and a little dazed at the end of it.

To Sally's immense shock and Bunny's embarrassed delight, since the wags in the clubs had no difficulty calculating the date of the event, she found some weeks later that she was expecting a child. It was an ordeal being with child at her advanced age, and the doctors shook their heads with doubt. But nine months later she was delivered of a healthy baby boy. He was named Beauchamp Redcliffe Joliffe the Second, called Beau, for, as Sally said to Sophy, "I cannot have two Bunnies in the house!"

She had never been so happy. At long last she had given Bunny the son he had always wanted, and he treated her with respectful admiration and often, love. While it would be a fairy tale to imagine he never had another mistress, Bunny certainly became a good deal more attentive to his wife and he never went back to Virginie.

Once she saw that her plans had come to nothing, and many were blaming her for the whole incident, Virginie left London forever. She went to the Continent, where her very English complexion and generous figure quickly found her a series of male companions. None however, talked of marriage until the Baron de Verville, a man in his late fifties, made her an offer she felt she would be foolish to refuse. He had escaped the worst of the ravages of the Revolution by growing his hair and beard, and pretending to be his own valet. He was wise enough to hide his money and other valuables in waxed sacks under the privies. As a member of the downtrodden classes, he had been able to stay in his château, though at times perforce sharing it with bands of revolutionaries wearing the tricolor on their arms and terrifying him with their violent rhetoric.

When the Revolution was over he had waited a while, shaved and cut his hair, and then emerged once more as Monsieur le Baron. Not surprisingly, his experiences had made him both cautious and old before his time. He wanted a pretty wife to care for him, but he did not want to be cuckolded. In his youth it had been commonplace for the nobility to have contractual agreements between those proposing marriage. These laid out their private lives in some detail. He therefore had Virginie sign a contract stipulating that she would receive him in her bed twice a month, at his pleasure, and promise never to take a lover, even if her husband fell into dotage. If she kept to this contract she would have all the rights and privileges of Madame la Baronne. If not, she would be cut off without a sou. Once she got over the pleasure of being titled and not having to worry about money, it was hard for Virginie to be reduced to a poorly-performing lover twice a month, especially when there were so many handsome, virile chevaliers who would gladly have provided her with the pleasures she missed. But her husband had an eagle eye and informants everywhere. She was forced into a virtual celibacy which, as the Baron descended into a feeble old age, became a real one. By the time he died, having lived far longer than she had hopefully expected, she had put on flesh and lost her looks. No one wanted her anymore. She was rich and comfortable, but alone.

After leaving Charles, Lysander walked home, running the whole scene over and over in his mind. He had found it almost intolerable. Asking to shake the hand of a man he despised was the hardest thing he had ever done. He could only imagine the ribald and vulgar comments that were even now being passed from ear to ear. He felt he had shamed not only himself but the whole House of Hale.

In this he was wrong, since the comments were largely in his favor. Everyone admired him for taking all the blame on himself and protecting Sally's name. His admiration of her raised her standing amongst the *ton* and she afterwards found herself sought out by people who had previously ignored her. But for his lordship, the whole affair had been an unmitigated disaster. He vowed never to set foot in Brooke's again and to remove his family to Hale Court in Buckinghamshire as soon as possible.

When he arrived home, he went straight into the ballroom. He lit a candelabra, swearing like a sailor when the candles would not take immediately, and carried it to the pianoforte. He threw off his coat and neckcloth, pulled off his pocket watch and undid his waistcoat by the expedient of ripping off all the buttons, which scattered loudly all over the parquet. He sat himself at the piano. He rifled through all the sheet music, letting it drop to the floor, until he found the most difficult piece he had. Then he proceeded to play as loudly as he could, at first rather badly, but with increasing skill, the Beethoven's Piano Concerto No. 5. The whole house rang with it. If he had been afraid that Sylvester's banging would ruin the instrument, he had no thought of that now. He played with such force and passion that sweat was soon stinging his eyes and his fingers were slippery on the keys.

He played it all the way through then began again, so that by the time Sophy came downstairs he had been at the piano for over an hour. She was in bed when he had started to play and recognized the violence with which he was attacking the keys. Her heart had gone out to him. She knew how hard the apology would have been for him and longed to take him in her arms. But he needed to exorcise his demons in his own way. But now the playing had become less violent and in any case, she could bear to leave him no longer. She came quietly into the ballroom and stood in the shadows waiting for him to finish.

As the last notes died away and he dropped his head into his arms, she came up behind him and put her arms around him. He was wet with sweat and his heart was pounding. He turned to face her and in what seemed like one swift movement, stood, kicked away the piano bench, closed the lid over the keys, pulled her nightgown up to her waist and lifted her so she was balanced on the edge of the closed piano. She let him do it, knowing this was one way she could help him. Holding her there with one hand, he undid the buttons on his trousers and plunged into her. For some minutes there was no sound in the ballroom but their heavy breathing and then Lysander's groan. Then there was complete silence.

"Oh God, Sophy, I'm so sorry," he said, looking at her with such despair in his eyes that it brought tears to hers. He let her go and her feet slid to the floor. "I'm so sorry. I don't know what..."

"Shh, it's all right" hushed Sophy, holding him tightly. "It's all right. There's nothing to be sorry about. I love you. It's all right."

They remained like that for a minute or two, until he suddenly gave a shuddering sigh and lifted his head. She looked up into his face. "It's over now," she said quietly. "We are never going to mention it again. It's over." And she kissed him. "Come to bed now, my darling. Come."

CHAPTER SEVENTEEN

In which the Earl makes plans for the future.

The next morning, Lysander awoke before his wife and lay for some time thinking about the events of the previous day and a half. By sheer willpower, he had held in his emotions until he could do so no longer. Then for the first time in his adult life he had simply given in to an impulse without thinking at all. Now, though, it was as if a person other than he had lived through it all. He remembered the shameful Apology, coming home and playing the piano and then... Sophy, holding him, telling him that everything was all right. An immense relief had washed over him. This morning he felt as if he had somehow been through fire and come out purified.

As if sensing that he was thinking about her, Sophy stirred. He turned onto his side to look at her and began to curl one of her long strands of hair around his finger. The curl clung to the finger and as he tried to remove it, he must have pulled her hair, because she frowned a little and opened her eyes. When she saw him, she smiled sleepily.

"Your curl captured my finger," he said. "It won't let go."

"Mmm... my curls do have a mind of their own," replied Sophy, awaking more fully, "like that woman, what was her name, who had snakes for hair."

"The Gorgon," said her husband. "She turned men to stone. Not such a bad comparison - you turn a certain part of me to stone." He gave a sad smile. "I'm so sorry about last night, Sophy," he said quietly. "I can't think what happened to me. I don't know what to say."

"Say nothing, especially not that you're sorry. I'm the one who should be sorry. I forced you into a situation that caused you great pain. I love you and I should do everything I can to protect you. That is *my* honor and I didn't uphold it. So, no apology, no discussion."

Suddenly, a demanding little voice could be heard, and without warning the door to Sophy's bedroom was flung open.

"Papa!" said the heir, "I want, I need..."

"What did I tell you about coming into people's bedchambers without knocking?" said Lysander. "Go outside immediately and knock to be admitted."

"But Papa, I want..."

"No buts. Outside immediately. Knock and wait for someone to say come in. If no one says come in, perhaps they didn't hear your knock. Then you say 'May I come in?' and wait for the answer."

And as his son began to expostulate, his lordship added severely, "I will not say it again. Outside at once, sir, and do not dare to come in until you are bid!"

The boy left the room, his little chin set in an expression so like his mother's that in spite of himself, Lysander had to smile. They heard a knock, and Sophy started to answer, but her husband stopped her.

"Let him wait. Dammit, we can't have him coming in like this all the time with no let or hindrance."

A small voice with more than a hint of annoyance said, "I come in now?"

"No!" replied the Earl. "We are not ready to receive you. Wait."

"Let the poor little boy come in!" whispered Sophy. "He's been very good!"

"Tell me again you forgive me, and I shall," responded her husband.

"I already told you, there's nothing to forgive. You did what you had to do, what I forced you into, even though it went against every instinct in your body. I'm the one needing forgiveness."

When Lysander made a demur, she said as lightly as she could, "Oh, just let's forget all about it!" Then she called, "You may come in, darling!" and when their son ran to the bed, she helped him up. "Now, what did you want to ask?"

"I need 'nother sword, for Daisy," announced the young knight. "I can't killed her if she don't have no sword. Not gent'man."

"Quite right!' responded the Earl seriously. "A gentleman does not kill an unarmed opponent. It is not honorable. I'm very glad you realize that. I shall ask the carpenter to make you another sword." Then he continued, "You may kiss your Mama now if you wish, but Sylvester, a gentleman does not go into people's bedchambers without knocking. That is not honorable either. I hope I don't have to tell you this again. Understood?"

His son nodded.

"Where is Daisy, anyway?" asked the Earl.

"She getting my breakfast," answered his son, "but I don't yike porridge. I want muffins!"

"Go down and tell her that your Mama says if you eat three spoons of porridge you may have a muffin."

"Two muffins? I have two muffins?" asked the boy, looking earnestly at them with the blue eyes that won his father's heart and the smile that won his mother's.

"Oh, very well," they said in unison, and, glancing at each other, laughed.

Not wanting to hear any of the gossip about the events of the last few days, Lord and Lady Hale cancelled all but the most intimate social engagements until their departure for Hale Court. For the next week or so, they drove together in the park, ate lunch and dinner at home and played piquet in the evenings. Sophy remarked that it reminded her of when they were first married, except that then they did not have the young Sylvester who seemed to appear every time his lordship took his wife in his arms. The one lingering effect of the Earl's raging outburst seemed to be that his son could hardly bear to have his father out of his sight.

They would take Winton, Susan and Daisy with them to the Court but the rest of the London staff would stay behind. The Court had its own full complement. During their four-month absence the London house would be meticulously cleaned and any repairs made. One early result of this was that when her ladyship walked into her bedchamber several days before their removal, she found her roses and cherubs bed missing. Annoyed, she ran downstairs to her husband's study. He was looking at some papers with his feet up on his desk. He swung his long legs down and stood up as she came in, as he always did.

"What have you done with it?" she said in some heat and without preamble, "my bed, what have you done with it?"

"The frame is at a foundry being copied in cast iron," said her husband calmly. "The head and footboard will be attached when it's ready. I don't think even we will be able to break that."

"Oh," said Sophy, the wind taken out of her sails, "but why didn't you tell me? I thought you'd had it chopped up, as you said you would."

"Because, my hot-headed beloved, I didn't know you had come home! I asked my excellent secretary James to look into having a cast iron frame made while we are away, but for what will prove no doubt to be an excellent reason, he arranged for the bed to be picked up today." He came forward and put his arms around her. "Sophy! You don't really think I would destroy your bed, knowing how much you love it, do you? Do you think so badly of me?"

"No, of course not! I know you would never be so unkind. I was just cross on the instant. It was silly." Sophy buried her head in her husband's shoulder. "I'm sorry! I seem to lose my temper easily at the moment. Perhaps it's because I haven't been feeling in prime twig these past few days."

"Hmm," said her husband looking at her doubtfully. "Are you sure you feel up to the removal to the Court next week? We can delay it, if you like."

"No, I'm sure I'll be better by then. No need to throw a rub in the way of our going. Sylvester is so looking forward to it. Anyway, I have no bed! Wherever shall I sleep?" She looked at him under her lashes.

Her husband raised an eyebrow. "I can make a small space for you in my bed, I imagine, even though your bottom has grown so large."

"No! It hasn't, has it?" Sophy, twisting around, attempted to see her derrière in the mirror.

Her husband looked serious. "I think it requires closer examination. He moved over to her and patted the object of the discussion. "Yes, definitely more examination required." He kissed her fondly.

As if on cue, the study door was flung open and Sylvester marched in. "Papa…" He noticed the position of his father's hands. "Why you holding Mama's *bottom*?" He whispered the last word, having been told that one did not discuss certain parts of the body in public.

"*Because,*" whispered his father, "*Mama is afraid it's too big.*"

"I yook," he said, stalking over to his mother and examining her behind. "'Snot too big," he said decidedly, forgetting to whisper. "Mama, your bottom 'snot too big."

"Good man!" said his father. "That's what I think, too."

"Thank you, gentlemen," Sophy curtseyed. "But my (whispered) *bottom* is not what you came in for, is it, Sylvester?"

"Papa," said their son anxiously. "Is my 'nother sword made? Mr. Peter (the carpenter) tooked my own sword away and now I gots no sword at all. I reely need my sword for going to the Court!"

"Of course you do! Ask Daisy to take you to Mr. Peter's workshop. I imagine it's ready by now. He is very clever. He has several times repaired the bed that Mama broke with her big bottom."

But his son heard neither the end of the sentence, nor Sophy's cry of outrage. He had already left. The Earl laughed at his wife's indignation and kissed her.

"You are such a beast and a tease!" complained Sophy when she could speak. "I don't know why I love you so much." She nuzzled her face in his shoulder. Then, breaking away, she said, "Oh, I must tell you. I saw Sally Joliffe in the park. I know I said we would never discuss it, and we won't, but she asked me to tell you how grateful she is to you. I don't know what you said, but it seems to have had a real effect on Bunny. He has never appreciated her so much, she says. Of course, she was discrete, but from what she said I believe they've... let's say, renewed their relationship. He's not seeing Virginie any more, apparently. She's gone – for good, it seems. I thought you would like to know. I know the whole episode was dreadful for you, but good has come out of it."

"I'm glad," replied her husband. "Sally deserves better than she has. He isn't worthy of her. But don't let's talk about either of them any more."

Abruptly changing the subject, he said, "By the way, I, or I should say, James, has just completed the purchase of

Fielding House on Park Lane. I'm sorry I didn't tell you before, but I had to move fast. It came up for sale and I heard Monty Burnham was sniffing around it. I was damned if I'd let him have it. According to Weatherby, James ran rings around him – he'll go far in politics, that boy! Poor Fielding was a nice old chap. Had two wives who both died in childbirth and he never tried again after that. But he was the last of the line so when he died the place was put on the market. He lived pretty much in seclusion for the last twenty years and it needs refurbishment, but it's an Adam Brothers townhouse and I thought it would make a good Dower House."

"A Dower House? For whom?"

"For you, of course. I've seen what a nonsense it is for Charles and Georgianna to uproot his mother from London, and I don't want the same to happen to you. I don't believe Sylvester would ever do anything to make you unhappy, but it will pose a problem when I'm gone. Sylvester and the new Countess will want to move in here. I've always thought it iniquitous that widows should be sent away to the country and lose not only their home but also their society. My mother would never have gone to the Dower House at Hale Court. Thank God I never had to try to make her go there. I did think of buying a London house for her at the time, but since I wasn't married, it never became necessary. The Dower House at the Court has been empty for years, so we'd better look at that, too. When the time comes, you'll need somewhere to go when you want to get out of the city."

Sophy could not speak. The idea of Lysander dying was more than she could bear and her eyes filled. Her husband saw her tears and said in some alarm. "But I'm just looking out for your future! Now you'll have a place of your own to escape to when you're vexed with me!"

"I can't bear to think of being without you! Please don't talk about it! I don't want a Dower House!" she sobbed, her emotions getting the better of her. "I'll never be vexed with you again! Don't ever leave me, Lysander!"

He gave her one of his ever-present handkerchiefs and held her close. "I will never leave you, my love, you know that," he said. Then, hoping that outrage would replace her tears, he added, "And don't say you'll never be vexed with me again! One of my favorite things is when you're cross! You order me out of your room, or flounce out of mine, telling me not to come near you, so I leave you overnight and the next morning you jump into my bed and make passionate love to me."

"I do Not! And I don't flounce!" she retorted, as he hoped she would. But it was true she could never stay cross with him for long and it did usually end as he described, so she amended with a sniff, "not always!" She blew her nose and lay her head on his shoulder, and he kissed her cheek with a chuckle.

Then a thought occurred to her. "We could offer the Dower House to Charles for his mother. Then she wouldn't have to leave London, and Delia could stay in town for when James finally decides to ask her to marry him. What's the matter with him, anyway, why is he taking so long?"

His lordship pondered a minute before he spoke, then he said slowly, "You know, my love, that is a splendid idea, if I can persuade Charles to take it."

"Just tell him I refuse to have anything to do with a Dower House in London, which is true, and he would be doing you a favor by having his mother live there. It's bad enough having the one at Hale Court standing empty."

"You, my love, are as much a politician as James. Who, by the way, will propose to Delia when he's good and ready. Unlike me, he doesn't believe asking a woman to be his wife without careful forethought." He kissed her cheek again.

She made a face at him. "Leaving aside that dubious assertion, what would they live on? Surely he can't support a wife on a secretary's salary."

"If he decides to stay in my employ after his marriage, I would, of course, increase his remuneration as required for a married man, but you know he's talked about a career in politics and if he wants, I'll propose him for the next vacant seat in Buckinghamshire. I have a good deal of influence there, you know."

Since the Earl of Hale's estates covered about a third of the county, and he was a much-loved landlord, Sophy could readily believe this. "Hmm..." she said, swallowing a smile, "I think I shall have to have a word with him. He cannot keep Delia waiting around like this."

"Sophy, you will do no such thing!" cried his lordship, holding her at arms' length. "I absolutely forbid it! Leave James alone!"

His wife looked up at him and laughed. "Now you know how it feels to be teased! Of course I shall say nothing to James!"

She did not add, because she knew her husband would object vociferously, but if James did propose, and Delia accepted, she would certainly take her to Marianne for instruction, but warn her not to say "Marianne says" in intimate situations. She had learned that lesson.

A day or so later Charles and Georgianna came to a quiet dinner at Hale House. When the ladies left the men to their port and went into the sitting room, Georgianna said confidentially,

"Charles said we were not to speak of anything to do with the Apology, so, of course, I didn't mention it at dinner, but I have to tell you, Sophy! Apparently everyone is saying Lysander was marvelous and looked like a Prince, so dignified, you know. And he entirely blamed himself, said Sally was the best-looking woman in London and," she finished in a rush, "he admires her more than any woman except you!"

"Goodness!" said Sophy, not knowing quite how to respond. "I'm relieved no one is making fun of it all. He hates ridicule, not so much for himself, but for the family name." She did not want to say more on that topic, and continued, "I saw Sally in the park, and she has never been happier! Bunny has given up Virginie and they have had a reconciliation. I'm so glad for her. Not that I have any sympathy for him. It must be awful to have a husband who... likes other women!" They sat quiet for a moment in contemplation. "How lucky we are!"

"Yes," sighed Georgianna, "we are."

The two men came in laughing, as usual, and the conversation became general.

Later when they were in bed, Lysander said, "I put your suggestion to Charles, and he needed to be persuaded, but I told him what you had said, and he finally agreed. He insists on paying rent, though I'd rather he didn't. But I'll use the rent to do the renovations, so it will be to his mother's benefit in the end."

"I know I shouldn't ask, but what *is* Charles' financial situation. Is he plump in the pocket, or…?"

"Of course, I don't know in detail, but I believe it is… reasonable. His father was ill for a long time, as you know, but he wouldn't let Charles take over the management of the estates. His bailiff seems to have managed well enough, but it will take him some time to sort things out."

"You know, Lysander, when you offered to take me in place of my father's debt…"

Lysander interrupted, protesting, "Sophy, you know that's not…"

But she persisted, "When, as I say, you more or less bought me for, what was it - two thousand pounds? - my father told me you were the richest man in England. I've never known, was that true? Is that true?"

Her husband looked at her. "I wish I could convince you that I didn't *buy* you, as you always claim! I merely shortened the odds of your accepting me."

"Now you make me sound like a horse!"

"Dammit, Sophy!" said her husband with a half laugh of frustration, "I can see I'm never going to get the better of this argument. Anyway, to answer your question, with you and Sylvester, of course I'm the richest man in London, but I know that's not what you meant. One doesn't usually discuss finances with a lady, but…"

"Why ever not?" Sophy cried. "Why should we *ladies* not know such things? It concerns us, doesn't it? You talked today about what will happen to me after you're gone. But what if, God forbid, it should happen sooner than we think, while Sylvester is still a child, what then?"

"Then our people will help you. Mr. Weatherby you already know, and my agent and bailiffs will all be there."

"I'm sure they will, but it would be much better for me if I knew something about our circumstances in advance. And I'd much rather hear it from you."

His lordship sat up. "I'd prefer to do this in my office, where I could show you the records, but very well. Our income is derived essentially from two sources. Bank investments and our estate. What we have in the bank is our capital. The bank pays us interest which can vary quite widely from year to year. It's about five percent at the moment. If left alone the capital will increase, slowly but surely, because the interest compounds. I could show you it mathematically, if you like."

Sophy shook her head. "I don't need the details. I take your word for it, professor!"

Her husband laughed. "You sound just like Charles, when I did his prep! Anyway, to continue: if revenue from the farms is less than expected, or if we have unexpected calls on our purse, like buying the Dower House, I use some of the interest to meet those expenses. But I never touch the capital. Using one's capital or putting money in unsound investments is a sure road to financial ruin. Just a couple of years ago, a number of people put money into the development of a supposed new country in Central America. The man running the swindle was a Scott called MacGregor. He even wrote a book about it, even with illustrations, but it was all a total invention. When people who had invested went to find the place, there was nothing but jungle. Never invest in anything Weatherby doesn't approve of. He's a sound fellow."

"Did he approve of your investing in Marianne?" asked his wife, demurely.

"No he didn't! He strongly advised against it, and when I suggested he visit her to see what type of woman she was, he nearly had an apoplexy!" Lysander laughed at the memory. "But I owed her a great deal, so I didn't really care if I lost my money. But that was different."

"Of course it was, my dear," replied Sophy with a chuckle. "Anyway, professor, carry on."

"The other and major part of our income is derived from the land," continued the Earl, "We own about a hundred thousand acres in Buckinghamshire, largely leased to tenant farmers as you know, because you've met many of them. Most of the families have been on the Hale lands for generations. I run one small farm myself because I like to try out new ideas before encouraging the tenants to implement them. We've changed the crop mix from wheat and barley to wheat and rye, and we plant turnips on fields that used to lie fallow. Now we grow clover to feed larger herds of livestock in the spring and summer, and give them the turnips in the winter. We also grow far more potatoes than we used to. I tried it out on my farm and when the tenants saw it working, they did the same. These men are experts; they've lived on that land all their lives and I don't like to tell them what to do. But if I show them something works, they usually choose to follow. Farming went into recession when Bonaparte starting chasing us all across Europe. In fact, I bought up acreage from neighbors who failed, but we've weathered the storm and things are looking up now."

His lordship suddenly seemed to realize that all of this was a much longer answer than Sophy had asked for. "So, my love," he said, "to finally answer your question, I know I'm the richest man in England, but it has nothing to do with money. What I have in you and Sylvester is beyond any valuation." He kissed her cheek. "But the estate derives about seventy-five thousand pounds a year from farming. It should be higher, more like a pound an acre, but with the recession we're doing as well as we can. We have to pay taxes, of course, but that's what supports our two households and keeps you in those ravishing bonnets."

"Good gracious!" said Sophy wonderingly, "I had no idea! How do you do it all? No wonder you spend so much time in your office reading and looking at rows of figures! But how did you learn about it? Did your father explain it all to you when you were younger? Will you explain it to Sylvester?"

"The farming came to me naturally as I spent so much time at the Court when I was a boy. I used to talk to all the farmers and I like to read about agriculture. As far as finance is concerned, my father depended a lot on his man of business, who was Weatherby's father. He himself didn't have much of a head for figures. So I learned most of it from Weatherby Senior and from looking at all the records. You know I like anything to do with numbers. As for Sylvester, we'll have to see. He seems to have a very warlike disposition, which is usually incompatible with business, but I was very encouraged today by his finding it ungentlemanly to kill Daisy if she didn't have a sword, so there's hope! For myself, I think I was born to be an accountant. Not very thrilling, is it?"

"I find you very thrilling," said Sophy, putting her arms around her husband's neck. "You seem to be able to do everything." She kissed him.

"There are some things I'm particularly good at," replied her husband, "and they have to do with figures of a different sort. Here, let me show you." He slipped her nightgown off her shoulders and proceeded to demonstrate.

CHAPTER EIGHTEEN

In which the Hales remove to Buckinghamshire

At the end of May, the Hale family removed to Buckinghamshire. It was quite a caravan. The Earl and Countess travelled in her blue-lined carriage, while their son, much to his disgust, was put with Daisy, Susan and Winton in another. Jeb followed in the curricle. The coach came last, carrying what seemed like a mountain of luggage. Sylvester had lobbied for taking the high-perch phaeton and driving it himself. Neither parent could forbear laughing at his furious and mulish expression when he was told that not only could he not drive the vehicle, but under no circumstances could he even climb up into the dangerous conveyance. In any case, they were not taking it to the Court.

"Why you not take the perch-ton, Papa?" he demanded to know, his angelic face in a fierce frown. "All the 'nother carriages is ... is *cat lap.*" This ugly expression was one the boy had recently learned from his Uncle Charles when he teased him for drinking milk. His father decided he would have to have words with Charles the next time he saw him.

"Moderate your language, sir," replied his father, as his mother giggled behind her hand, "and do not question my decisions. The phaeton is of no use in country lanes and I know that sooner or later you would contrive to climb up onto it and break your neck. Go and sit with Daisy and leave your mother and me in peace for five minutes. You may come into our carriage after luncheon in Feyreham."

The stopping place for the family was her ladyship's home. The others would drive straight to the Court, changing the horses and lunching in Chesham. Hawthorne House had been in a sad state of repair when Lysander first met Sophy first met, but had since undergone major refurbishment, thanks to the Earl. Her father still lived there, still drank too much port and still gambled away more than he could afford. But the housekeeper Mrs. Peters and her son Robin kept the house, as she put it, *up to snuff*, hiring extra help from the village when necessary. The Hale family typically stopped there for luncheon on their way to and from the Court.

Sophy's father was rather afraid of his son-in-law, and they found that longer visits drove him to the bottle even more. So Sophy had taken Sylvester there without her husband two or three times and this had proved more successful. Unaccountably, their son was drawn to his grandfather, who behaved with much more than usual propriety when Sylvester was there. The two could often be found talking together. Whether either had any inkling of what the other was saying was doubtful, as her father was uncommunicative and elliptical at best, and Sylvester had always used words in his own idiosyncratic fashion. The key was, Sophy realized, that her father talked to her son exactly as he would to another man. He made no allowances at all for his age. This exactly suited Sylvester who did not relish being called a little boy or being treated like one.

The heir had also formed a fast bond with Robin, the housekeeper's son. He was mentally only a little more than the boy's age. Robin would show him birds' nests and baby rabbits, teach him how to whistle through grass and, unknown to his mother, help him to climb into the lower branches of trees. So Sylvester had two playmates, one who treated him like a man and one who did not know the difference. It was all enormous fun, and when he tumbled out of the carriage at Hawthorne House, he greeted the occupants with real joy.

After luncheon, during which Sylvester was allowed to sit at table with the adults, he proved to be capable of bearing the brunt of the conversation with his talk of swords, floating wood, boats and monkeys, all of which appeared to fascinate his grandfather Hawthorne. After luncheon, his lordship went for a walk around the property to investigate the latest repairs, especially the stables, where his fine team had been put to feed and rest. Sophy walked to the vicarage to see her old friend Mrs. Bradshaw, and Sylvester disappeared with Robin. Mr. Hawthorne fell asleep in the study under a week-old newspaper. Shortly after three in the afternoon they climbed into the carriage, where Sylvester, a good deal dirtier than he had been when they set out from London, promptly fell asleep.

"Oh dear," said his mother, "whatever will they think at the Court when he arrives in that state?"

"They will think he is a little boy who has had a great deal of fun," said her husband. "All the women will fight with each other as to who can bathe him, and all the men will nod wisely and say 'a bit o' dirt never 'urt nobody.'"

Lysander so perfectly imitated the country folk that Sophy burst out laughing, threw her arms around his neck and kissed him. The grubby boy in question woke about an hour later, and was inclined to be fussy, as most children are when they awaken from a nap. But his Mama took him on her knee and soon interested him in the sights they passed, creating stories about the people and animals. Thus, the happy family chatted and laughed its way through the countryside until they were driving through the arched gateway that pierced the walls of the demesne of Hale Court.

The whole household was outside to greet them as their carriage swept around the gravel path in front of the huge Gothic oak double door. The Court had been built in the mid-1500s by the first Earl who liked what he thought of as the Old English look. It was a large building with a medieval air, three stories high with a highly decorated roofline bearing a parapet, gables and turrets. It was built of deep red brick, with white stone outlining the large mullioned windows and the front door, and serving as contrast to the brick along the roofline.

In the tradition of many of the fine houses built at that time, it was in the shape of an E, with a long perpendicular wing at each end and a shorter center one. It was said that this style was to encourage Queen Elizabeth to stay there during her summer rounds, but there was no evidence that this had ever happened at Hale Court.

The warm red brick glowed though the leaves of the Virginia creeper covering a good deal of the façade, now tinted gold by the sinking sun of the early summer evening. Unusually for a home of this style, the area in front of the house was not a large lawn, but a rose garden laid out in four large squares surrounded by low box hedges. Inside each of the squares were four smaller rectangles of close-cut lawn enclosing a variety of rose bushes, now in bloom and perfuming the evening air. In the center of all was a large fountain featuring Neptune and spouting dolphins. The plash of the water on the marble basin could be heard against the call of the swallows returning to their nests.

The roses had been the passion of the Earl's great-great-grandmother and were as much a feature of the Hale family as the script H found everywhere carved into the oak paneling inside the house. The fireplace surrounds were all deeply carved with representations of local flora and fauna. Outside, nature was rampant in the flowers and the creepers, so in spite of its size, the house was welcoming rather than imposing. Sophy loved it.

A footman opened the door of the carriage. Sylvester was the first to leap down. Oblivious to the audible whisper of many voices from the rest of the staff who had not seen him in over six months, to the effect of how he had grown, how like his mother he was, what a handsome chappie he was, he immediately began interrogating Fotherington, the butler, who was at the head of the staff line.

"Fother'nton, Fother'nton," he cried, "is 'nother sword in nurs'ry? I gots two but Papa says…"

He was interrupted sternly by his father. "Sylvester! Is that any way to greet Fotherington? Where are your manners, sir?"

His son stopped and searched his memory for an appropriate greeting. Then, with a bow, he said to the butler, "'Vester Barrington, 'tyour service."

This was met with a titter from those of the staff who heard it, and a murmur as it was reported to those who had not. Fotherington remembered the present Earl when he was Sylvester's age, and his demeanor lost none of his stateliness. He bent to the young lord and replied,

"Thank you, young master. But you do not need to bow to me. You may shake my hand like this." He took the boy's right hand and, suiting the word to the action, said, "Good evening, Fotherington, I trust I find you well."

"G'evening, Fothern'ton, I tust find you well," repeated the boy.

"Thank you, I am very well," replied the butler with enormous dignity. "Now, may I help you with something? You were asking…?"

"My 'nother sword? I gots two but my Papa says 'nother one is in nurs'ry."

"I'm afraid our son is showing signs of a very warlike disposition," intervened his father, coming forward with her ladyship on his arm. "He has two wooden swords but is looking for yet another one I unwisely told him may be in the nursery. But I see Daisy waiting and she will deal with it."

He signaled to Daisy, who came forward and took the boy by the hand and led him away, still talking.

His lordship turned to the elderly butler. "Thank you, Fotherington. Good evening, and I trust we find you well?" He smiled. "Did you have to teach me in the same way?"

"Lord bless you, my lord, I was just a footman in those days and I don't imagine I spoke to you at all!" He bowed to her ladyship. "I hope you are not too fatigued after your journey, my lady? Will you rest before dinner? Shall I have tea brought up to your bedchamber?"

"Thank you, Fotherington. That would be very kind. I am unaccountably tired."

Sophy moved down the line, greeting the other members of staff who were now well known to her. Then she crossed the spacious stone-flagged hall, its ancient oak paneling darkly illuminated by the dying rays of the sun shining through the mullioned windows, and climbed the wide staircase to her bedchamber.

She could never arrive at the Court without remembering her wedding day when she came there for the first time. It had been an anxious time, and the introductions had seemed interminable. She had hardly been able to swallow a taste of the dinner specially prepared by the cook, and she had been unnerved by the footmen and maids who waited to serve her every need. Now it was all familiar to her. Now it was home.

She found Susan waiting for her in her bedchamber and her tea arrived soon after. She thankfully allowed her maid to remove her bonnet, travelling cloak and gown.

"I think I will rest for a moment,' she said. "I don't know why I am so tired. I've spent most of the day sitting down!" She sank gratefully onto her bed in her petticoat and in two minutes was asleep, her untouched tea growing cold on the stand next to her. Susan pulled a coverlet over her and crept out.

When her husband came into the room sometime later he kissed the curls peeping over the top of the coverlet, but did not disturb her. He dressed for dinner, and when she was still asleep an hour later, he went alone to see Sylvester put to bed.

His son was standing on his little bed brandishing the third sword, which, joy of joys, had been found in one of the cupboards. As his father came close, he lunged forward and would have fallen if his lordship had not caught him.

"If you're going to play with swords," he said, "you must learn not to lunge at people like that without warning, and certainly not to do it without standing firmly on two feet. Now get off the bed and stand here. Do as I do."

His father took up one of the other wooden swords, adopted the correct stance, and bringing the sword up in front of his face, said, "You must warn your opponent you are going to attack. You say *en garde* and then you may lunge. But you must have your back foot firmly planted. Watch."

He demonstrated a lunge. His son copied his words and movements exactly. Then they both did the same again several times.

"Now we'll practice a parry. Daisy, lunge towards me."

Daisy did so, at first alarmed at the idea of actually lunging towards the Earl, but then she copied the movements his lordship had just shown Sylvester.

"Look," the Earl said, "this is a parry," and parried her sword. They repeated the movement several times more.

"Now, you do the same with Daisy."

Sylvester parried Daisy's lunges perfectly.

"Excellent, my boy!" cried his lordship. "I think we've found something you've a talent for! Well done! Tomorrow I'll teach you the riposte, but now it is bedtime. No, no complaints. Let's say your prayers and I'll tell you a story."

In spite of vociferous objections and demands to know where his Mama was, the boy was inexorably tucked into his bed, insisting on keeping all his swords by his side. His father told the story of how Odysseus the sailor filled his men's ears with wax and had himself tied to the mast of his ship so as not to be lured onto the rocks by the beautiful singing of the Sirens.

"I not let my ship go on the rocks," declared the sixth Earl. "I yunge those Sirens with my sword! And I parry them!"

"No, they were too beautiful, and they sang lovely songs," replied his father. "They were irresistible, just like your Mama."

"Wass 'resistble?"

"IRResistible. That means you can't resist them. You have to do what they want. Now you have to do what I want, which is go to sleep."

"You 'resistble, Papa?" asked his son sleepily.

"I certainly hope your Mama thinks so. I'm going to see if she's awake. Goodnight, my very parfitt knight. Sleep well." He kissed his son on his curly head, and left.

However, when his lordship returned to his wife's bedchamber, he found her still fast asleep. Regretfully, he went downstairs, had a solitary glass of *fino* and dined alone.

"At least I have no competition for the almond tarts," he said to himself, remembering that these delicious pastries were the only thing Sophy had eaten at dinner on their wedding night. "But," he admitted, "I very yike Sophy... more than almond tarts. Much more." He smiled ruefully and ate another.

CHAPTER NINETEEN

In which Lysander meets an old friend

The following morning, Sophy woke with a start as she heard the huge old clock in the hall strike six. Still in her petticoat and her hair falling from its pins, she realized she had slept almost twelve hours. She sat up. Almost immediately, a wave of nausea hit her and she only just made it to the water closet before vomiting up what little was in her stomach. She sank to her knees beside the commode.

Suddenly she knew what had been making her weepy, irritable and, above all, tired these past few weeks. Of course! How would Lysander feel about having another child? She slowly rose to her feet, poured herself a glass of water and cleaned her teeth. She took the pins out of her hair and brushed it, reflectively. Feeling somewhat better, she went back to her bed, still thinking. It must date from the evening of the Apology and the piano incident.

There was a little plate of almond pastries next to the bed. As she nibbled one of them, she wondered who put them there. They really were delicious. Like Lysander, she remembered eating the same pastries on her wedding night, accompanied by two glasses of champagne. She smiled at the memory. She did not normally drink any alcohol and the champagne had made her quite dizzy. They had gone downstairs to receive the congratulations of the staff and then Lysander had brought her up here to her bedchamber. The next day he had left. How lonely and miserable she had been! It hardly seemed real now.

Thinking of those dreadful days made her desperate to see her husband, so she slid out of bed and ran through the communicating door into his room. He was sound asleep, so she slipped off her petticoat and chemise, climbed quietly into his bed and curled against him. She kissed his naked back. He made a murmur of pleasure, turned onto his back and put his arm around her.

"Good morning, my love," he said. "Do you feel rested after your long sleep?"

"A handsome Prince woke me with a kiss," she said.

"Since he obviously took away all your clothing and put you in here with me," replied her husband, "I'm torn between calling him out for kissing you, and shaking him gratefully by the hand." He kissed her lovingly. "Mmm… you taste of almond cakes."

"They were next to my bed."

"I know, I put them there. I ate my dinner in solitude and then brought them up for you. It was an act of purest altruism, as I was tempted to eat them all myself in my loneliness."

"I'm sorry! I just lay down for a moment and the next thing I knew it was morning."

A knock at the bedroom door and a familiar little voice interrupted them.

"Papa? I come in?"

"Already?" grumbled the Papa thus addressed, then loudly, "No! You may not come in! It's too early. Go back to bed!"

"But Papa! You said you teach me 'poste 'n the morning!"

"I do not teach the riposte or any other fencing before breakfast. Go away! Mama is sleeping."

"But Papa!" The little voice quavered, "I knock, like you say!"

"He *did* knock," whispered Sophy. "Let him in, please!"

Lysander groaned in despair. "Why am I tyrannized by a three-year-old? Oh, very well!"

He got out of bed, threw on his dressing gown and went to the door. He opened it and saw his son, barefoot, still in his night shirt, a suspicion of tears shining in his eyes.

"Papa!" The long-legged little boy thrust what he had in his arms at his father, his tears forgotten, his face all smiles. "I bringed my swords, yook!" Sure enough, there were all three swords. The little boy had carried them from the nursery at the far end of the west wing.

"But we can't do any fencing before breakfast," said his father. "And where's Daisy?"

"She sleepin'. I comed by mineself."

"Well, a gentleman doesn't fence in his nightshirt or before having something to give him strength, so let's go back to the nursery and get you dressed."

He put the swords under one arm and carried his son who chattered in a continuous stream of conversation about lunges and parries and ripostes until they arrived at the nursery. The door to Daisy's adjacent room was open, but inside was still in darkness.

Conscious of being clad in only his dressing gown, his lordship knocked on the door and called in, "Daisy, please get this young knight dressed and fed. He's demanding fencing lessons."

He then opened the nursery curtains to let in the first light of dawn now beginning to glimmer in the east. He exhorted his son to stay where he was till Daisy should appear and strode back to his bedchamber. Once there, he threw off his dressing gown and jumped into the bed.

"We have about ten minutes if we're lucky," he said to Sophy. "So no time for ancient Indian gymnastics, just plain, no nonsense…"

"Ancient Indian gymnastics? What are you talking about?" laughed Sophy, holding out her arms to him.

"It's an old book in the library. Can't understand a word of it. I think it's in Sanskrit. But it's got some very unusual illustrations. You'd like it. But right now there's something about knowing your son is waiting to attack you with swords that makes speed more important than novelty. I don't think the great lovers of history and legend ever had to deal with that. Stop giggling!"

"Well," panted Lysander a little more than ten minutes later, "I did warn you. And now you'd better remove into your own room as I'm going to ring for Winton. I have to prepare to instruct our fierce young son. No gentleman goes to a duel *en négligé*. I need to be appropriately garbed and breakfasted before I can face him."

Sophy laughed and scrambled out of his bed. "I'm still fascinated by the idea of those illustrations. Will you show me later?"

"Certainly, unless I'm lying on the cold earth, run through with wooden swords and you're left to the tender mercies of the sixth Earl. Didn't I say you'd be needing a Dower House?"

Still laughing, Sophy went through into her own room and rang for Susan, and the business of the day began.

When they came to their estate in the summer, it was the habit of Lord and Lady Hale to spend the first few days riding around the tenant farms. As he had told Sophy, Lysander was deeply attached to the lands that were his to manage and pass on to his son. He never felt as if he owned them; it might almost be said they owned him. He had grown up knowing that not only the land, but the lives of the many people who made their living on it, were his responsibility. He would repeat this circuit several times a year and in the autumn there would be a harvest feast at the Court for all those working on the estate.

This bright day had begun very early for the whole family. In spite of the substantial breakfast Sylvester had insisted on eating with his Papa, cutting a wide swathe through the sweet breads the cook had made specially for Sophy, and the lesson that followed, the morning would not have been far advanced when the party set off for the first of their visits, had it not been for the young lord's need for more sustenance after the swordplay with his father. He had escaped his Mama and Daisy, who were discussing his wardrobe, and had run to the kitchen, where, as well as a large slice of bread and jam, he had received the intelligence that there were kittens in the stables.

The mother cat was the fierce matriarch Sophy had sketched on her first trip to the Court. She regularly presented litters of kittens to the estate, with the result that the mouse and rat population of the barns and outbuildings was kept very low. Sylvester ran to the stables and would have leaped in among the kittens had not Jeb prevented him. The mother cat was not fond of anyone except Jeb himself, and certainly not of little boys with jam all over their face and a large slice of sticky bread in their hands. So the young lord decided to lie full length on the stable floor at some distance from the kittens, and try to coax them out by offering them his second breakfast, taking mouthfuls of it himself as encouragement. This did not succeed in its objective, but it did succeed in covering the front of his nankeens and jacket with straw, mud and the other less savory debris of the stable floor.

At length, frustrated by the kittens' continued inattention, he got up. His face bore substantial evidence of the jam he had enjoyed, and, as he tried to brush himself off, his sticky hands merely became covered with the undelicious mixture on his front. He ran back into the house, just in time to meet his mother and father coming downstairs ready for the outing. They both stopped, mouth agape, as they beheld the heir to the Earldom, his face and person filthier than any guttersnipe on the London streets, and emanating a distinct smell of manure.

The young man himself was oblivious to their astonishment. "Papa! Mama! There's kittens in the 'tables! But Jeb says not touch them. He says Mama cat skatch me! They didn't yike bread n' jam. I ate it mineself."

The Earl finally found words. "Fascinated as we are by your activities and even more by your appearance, Sylvester, we are due to leave immediately, so we do not have time to fully appreciate them." Turning to the butler he said, "Fotherington, please send for Daisy and ask her to perform some sort of miracle in ten minutes and render this… urchin presentable to the outside world."

Fotherington bowed and waved at one of the footmen, who hurried off. His lordship led his lady into the family drawing room and they sat down, looked at each other and burst out laughing. "H… how does he do it?" spluttered Sophy. "I saw him not thirty minutes ago and he was perfectly presentable."

"He is simply drawn to dirt, or rather, as he forges ahead, dirt sticks to him and he neither sees nor cares. It's rather wonderful, really. I have to say, I admire him."

Sophy laughed. "Were you like that when you were little?"

"Not a bit. I was always neat as a new pin. I've never liked getting dirty. He must have it as an inheritance from you. I imagine you were a grubby little girl with your curls sticking to your cheeks. I would have found you as admirable as I find Sylvester, but you would have found me an insufferable prig."

Sophy laughed again, and kissed him. "As a matter of fact, I was a very good little girl," she said. "My cheeks were not sticky and my curls were in order… well, most of the time. I did like to hang upside down from tree branches with Robin, until Mama told me it was unseemly to display my pantaloons in public."

"As I suspected," responded her husband with a kindling look. "I wish I could have seen you. I would have enjoyed the view of the pantaloons."

Before this conversation could continue in what would, no doubt, have been a not altogether appropriate vein, a magically changed Sylvester reappeared and the family set out.

His lordship drove the curricle at a sedate trotting pace, again resisting his son's attempts to take the reins.

"Sit quietly and look, Sylvester. Look at the fields. That one is barley. See how the ears have long straight hairs? It's green now but later on it will be like a golden ocean."

"Wass 'ocean', Papa?"

"It's a very wide stretch of water, so big you can't see across it. Big ships sail on it."

"Is rats in those big ships?"

"Yes, why?"

"I yike rats."

"Hmm, well, there are rats in the fields, too, you know."

"Where? I can't see no rats."

"You mean *any* rats. You can't see *any* rats. That's because they're hiding from the cat."

"Why?"

"Because the cat will eat them."

The child's eyes grew big. "Why?"

"Because that's what cats do. They eat mice and rats. You eat bread and jam. Cats eat mice and rats. But can we talk about the fields now, Sylvester? I don't know how we got on the subject of rats."

His son was quiet, which his lordship took for acquiescence. Mistakenly, as it soon appeared.

"You see all those rows of green leaves with white flowers? That's potatoes."

"Does rats eat 'tatoes?"

"Yes, rats eat just about anything."

"I yike 'tatoes, too. I give my 'tatoes to the rats and they be my friend and I say don't let cat eat you." He surveyed the potato field for a moment, then looked up at his Papa. "Thems not 'tatoes. 'Tatoes isn't green and white fowers!"

"The potatoes grow under the ground, under the green leaves. You have to dig them up."

"I yike digging!"

"I'm sure you do," sighed his father, giving up on the lesson in agriculture, "as it involves dirt."

"And probably rats," added his mother with a laugh.

They were destined for the village of Hale, which lay at a distance of about 15 miles from the Court at the crossroads in the center of the estate. There they would eat a simple lunch in the pub called, appropriately enough, *The Earl of Hale.* The road ran through one section of the Hale estate. The laborers in the fields, recognizing the Earl and his Lady on sight, stopped working and doffed their caps as they passed. The tenant himself would usually come to the hedgerow and, bowing to her ladyship, exchange a few words with his lordship on the state of the crops, the expected yield, and, of course, the farmer's best friend and worst foe, the weather.

As they passed the cottages, the women would come out, having been informed by a fleet-footed child that the lord and his lady were on their way. They would be offered refreshment: cool spring water or home-brewed beer. There would be dried flower and berry infusions for her ladyship, who was known to be a tea drinker. There were little playthings for Sylvester: a straw horse, a whistle made from a reed, a curiously shaped stick. Not being the sort of boy to hide behind his mother's skirts, and deriving genuine pleasure from these gifts, he charmed them all with his lovely smile and heartfelt thanks. When the curricle moved on, the tenants congratulated themselves on having their future assured by the young master. One and all, they declared him to be the image of his beautiful mother and a real gentleman like his father.

Progress was slow, and it was late morning before they arrived at the village pub, where both they and the horses would eat and rest. This was an ancient place, predating the Court. Either through age or by design, it was so sunk into the earth that they had to step down into the premises, and so low-ceilinged that his lordship had to constantly take care not to bang his head against the pitch-covered timbers. It was very dim, for the windows were small and mullioned, with old, almost opaque greenish glass. The stone walls were over a foot thick, so it was not only delightfully cool after the warmth of the day, but also very quiet. The only sound was the buzzing of a fly against one of the windows. A great peace settled immediately upon them and they found themselves talking in low voices, almost whispering.

They were served cheese and lamb from his lordship's own farms, together with little new potatoes, freshly dug, boiled up whole with mint and served with butter. Sophy, still a little queasy, ate sparingly, but as this was usual for her, it raised no comment. Lysander made up for it, as meat and potatoes with no vegetables was exactly his favorite type of meal. Sylvester ate a mountain of the little new potatoes swimming in butter until he declared that he had, in another of his Uncle Charles' expressions, "an ache in me pudding basin," and promptly fell asleep on one of the ancient oak wooden settles in the snug. His parents shook their heads over him, wondering, as parents will, where he had come from, amazed that they had produced this little piece of nature, so like and yet unlike themselves.

Their route home took them along one of the other roads out of the village, along which they passed more fields and farms, with the same greetings, stops and gifts. From the center of the village, the roads radiated out like the spokes of a wheel, all bordered on both sides by the Hale estate. It was possible to cut across the top of the fields to return to the Court along old cart paths that had probably been there since the time of the Romans. It was along one of these paths that the Hale family encountered an encampment of Romanys or gypsies, as they were often called. This itinerant group had been camping here for generations. They would come to help with the spring planting and return for the harvest. Their dwellings were a mixed lot of tents, carts and high painted wagons, like little wooden houses on big yellow wheels. Some of them were quite plain, but one or two were covered with highly decorated red panels. Lysander had known the Romanys since he was a boy, and now greeted by name the leader of the group who came forward, hand outstretched.

"Sastipe, Patrin!" said his lordship and gripped the other man's hand. "This is an unexpected pleasure! Still here? I hope I find you and your family well?"

"Sastipe, milor," replied the other, a short, dark man of a strong, stocky build, of about the same age as Lysander. "I am glad to see you again. Yes, we usually leave before this, but my wife gave me a fine son just one moon ago and according to our custom, she has been living apart. But the boy is now baptized and she has had the purification ceremony, so she can live with us again. We could not travel while she was still apart, it would bring very bad luck. We leave tomorrow, so it is well met, indeed! Please to come and see my son. I hope he and your boy will be friends as you and I have been."

They dismounted from the curricle and Patrin led them to one of the high, decorated wagons. "This is my *vardo*. My wife and boy are inside. Please to go in."

The top half of the door was already open, and he unlatched the bottom half so they could mount the steps and enter. The inside of the *vardo* was as ornate as the outside, the curved wooden sides and roof red with gold trim and painted with a profusion of flowers and fruits. There were benches on both sides and a trunk in the center, which probably served as a table. On the left side was clearly a kitchen area. There was a large pitcher of liquid, beer perhaps, a loaf, some sausages, potatoes and a stack of plates. A braided row of onions hung from a peg.

At the far end was a partitioned compartment from which a comely black-eyed young woman now emerged. She wore a full red and black skirt with a deeply fringed gold shawl tied around the waist and over her nicely rounded hips. A white embroidered bodice left the tops of her shoulders bare, and the hills of her plump bosom were clearly visible. Her abundant black hair was held back by a colorful kerchief and in her ears were large gold hoops. Sophy immediately felt old and dowdy in her pale blue superfine traveling ensemble with a long-sleeved fitted jacket trimmed with black braid, although when she had put it on that morning, she had thought it looked quite nice. Her perky bonnet had a blue feather, to be sure, but what was that compared with a red kerchief and gold hoop earrings? She stole a sideways look at her husband and saw him bow appreciatively and raise the new mother's little hand to his lips.

"Sylvester!" he said, "make your bow to Madame."

The little boy did as he was bid, bowing from the waist with his customary "'Vester Barrington, 'tyour service." This was met by a flood of speech from Madame, not a word of which was understood by anyone except her husband.

"I am sorry but my wife does not speak the English. She says that with those blue eyes and his beautiful face, so like his Mama, and the nose of his Papa, which tells of good things, his young lordship will have his pick of many women. He will have the opportunity to make many sons."

"Well," his lordship hesitated. "It is to be hoped that, while he may have his pick of many women, he will make sons with only one of them."

The Romany translated this for his wife and she laughed, then let forth another torrent of speech. This, however, her husband refused to translate, saying merely, "It is nonsense what my wife speaks, just the words of a woman. But, please to see my son, Danior."

He showed them to a wooden cradle next to the curtained partition in which lay a bonny baby with rosy cheeks, black eyes and black curly hair.

"Danior! What a beautiful name and what a beautiful baby!" exclaimed Sophy in delight. "His eyes are his mother's and his curly hair his father's. What a handsome man he will be! He won't have any problem finding a lovely wife, either. I'm sure you will have many grandchildren."

Patrin duly translated this for his wife who, smiling and chattering incomprehensibly, flew to Sophy, took her by the shoulders and kissed her on both cheeks. She did the same to Sylvester, who, to do him credit, took it stoically, and then she advanced on his lordship. Lysander gave every indication of looking forward to the embrace until a sharp word from her husband caused Madame to retreat. Instead, she gave him a brief curtsey. His lordship looked crestfallen.

Patrin then poured some dark liquid into four tiny jewel-colored glasses and handed them around, saying, "We drink to the health of my son, Danior."

They all raised their glasses, and his lordship said, "To Danior, may he have a long life, surrounded by those who love him and whom he loves. May he have a beautiful wife who will give him many sons and daughters and make him very happy. Danior, *t'aves baxtalo!*"

They all echoed "Danior, *t'aves baxtalo!*" and drank. The liquor was sweet, herb tasting and quite delicious. Then to Sophy's surprise and Sylvester's intense delight, Patrin and his wife, closely followed by Lysander, threw the glasses onto the wooden floor, where they smashed into a myriad of gem-like pieces. Seeing her ladyship's shock, their host said, "We do not wish a, how do you say, smaller toast to be in the glasses, so we break them."

"Oh, I see! How nice! What a good idea." Sophy made as if to break her glass, but found she could not cold bloodedly throw such a pretty thing to the floor, and rather shamefacedly put it down. Soon after, the Hale family left the happy couple and, getting back into the curricle, continued the drive home.

"It was so nice inside that... what was it... *vardo*," mused Sophy. "I wonder what it would be like to live like that... and I should like to dress like that, too," she added, half to herself.

"When I was a lad," said her husband nostalgically, "I wanted to run away with the gypsies. They didn't have those *vardos* then, just carts and tents, but it seemed so attractive to me. I liked the idea of leaving everything behind and rolling along in complete freedom."

"Especially," added his wife, "if you had a buxom consort like Patrin's by your side!"

"Especially so," agreed Lysander, twinkling at her.

"I yike that house," said Sylvester. "I yike to break the glasses!" He made a wild motion with his arm, accompanied by a crashing sound.

"Oh no you don't," said his Mama and Papa in unison, and laughed.

CHAPTER TWENTY

In which her ladyship enjoys a glass of wine

It was almost six in the evening by the time the Hale family returned to the Court. The gently waving leaves of the creeper covering the walls were tinted gold along the edges by the late afternoon sun and the bees were making their last forays amongst the roses. All three members of the Hale family were tired by the long day, and Sylvester was exhausted. His Papa carried him up to the nursery, where, after a few bites of supper and a quick wash, the boy could hardly keep his eyes open. When Sophy tucked him in bed he muttered, "I yike that house with big wheels," and immediately fell asleep.

My lord and his lady tiredly changed for dinner, both wishing they did not have to, but neither wanting to disappoint Mrs. Simmons, the cook, who took such special care to make all their favorite dishes during the first few days of their summer stay in the country. There was early asparagus from the hothouses, which Sophy loved and even Lysander, for whom vegetables were a duty rather than a pleasure, enjoyed. Whether he enjoyed it for its own sake, or from the titillation of watching Sophy suck her buttery fingers, is another question.

"If you don't stop putting your fingers in your mouth like that," he finally whispered to her, after sending the butler for more, unnecessary, wine, "I shall jump over the table and ravish you." Whereupon, she smiled and deliberately licked her fingers slowly with her tongue fully extended one last time. "Baggage!" he exclaimed and, rising from his seat, was halfway towards her just as Fotherington returned with a bottle from the cellars.

"This is the Sauternes you requested, my lord," said Fotherington entering, looking at the bottle a little puzzled, "but surely you do not wish it served with the meat?" Then, seeing his lordship on his feet, "Was there something you required, my lord?"

"No," replied the Earl, improvising madly, "I thought her ladyship had dropped an earring, but now I see it is not so. And no, the Sauternes is for the pudding. I thought there might be strawberries and... if there are, I wanted some..." his voice tailed off unconvincingly, as Sophy giggled.

"I believe there are strawberries, my lord. Shall I bring them now?"

"Absolutely, and see if there are any more almond tarts... and cream," commanded his lordship, searching for ways to keep the butler out of the room for as long as possible. "And where are those colored glasses, you know, the long-stemmed ones?"

"You don't mean the hock glasses, my lord? You wish to serve the Sauternes in those?" the butler sounded and was, scandalized.

"Yes, her ladyship likes them, so why should we not use them? Don't be such a stick-in-the-mud, Fotherington!" Thus his lordship adroitly passed responsibility to everyone but himself for this unwarranted request. Sophy, who rarely drank wine, hardly knew one wine glass from another, and poor Fotherington wondered whether he was missing some new London trend in the matter of wine glasses.

"Of course, my lord," he replied a little harassed, "whatever you wish, but it may take a minute or two to find them and make sure they are in order."

Since this was exactly what Lysander wanted, he answered airily, "No rush, no rush. I am still eating from this excellent joint. Please convey my felicitations to Mrs. Simmons on this marvelous meal." And he waved his hand in dismissal, an act wholly unlike himself.

The much imposed-upon butler departed. Sophy, fearing he might still be in earshot, smothered her laugh in her napkin. "You are awful, Lysander! The poor man! And what do you mean by waving your hand like that? It was just like one of those eastern potentates one occasionally sees at Court!" She waved her hand imperiously in the air.

In response, her unrepentant husband merely leaped from his chair, and coming round to her, pulled her from hers and into a crushing embrace. "It's your fault, sitting there, so beautiful, and inflaming me like that! I shall never be able to look at asparagus again without experiencing ... discomfort in my lower regions."

He unhooked the front of her evening dress, put his hand inside and kissed her breast. Her gown was a new one: a lovely low-cut ivory silk with cap sleeves, narrow below the bosom and falling into soft folds. It was embellished with rows of blue embroidery around the low neckline and the sleeves, and just above the hem. With it she wore her sapphire earrings and necklace. She was, as Susan had said, "a picture".

Sophy was torn between fending him off so he would not crush her new gown and giving in to the lovely feel of his warm hand. She was also aware that Fotherington could return at any minute, so finally she put her hands on both sides of his head and lifted it from her breast, kissed him on the lips and firmly pushed him away. "Behave yourself!" she said. "What would you say if Sylvester were to do such a thing at the dinner table. When he's grown up, of course!"

"I should congratulate him on his good taste and encourage him to continue," replied her husband, "which is more than *anyone*," he looked meaningfully at her, "will do for me!" Reluctantly, he returned to his seat.

Sophy had only just managed to re-hook the front of her gown and sit down, when Fotherington returned. He carried a tray which bore two lovely ruby-colored glasses, deeply etched, a bowl of strawberries, a small jug of cream and a plate of pastries.

"Oh, how pretty!" exclaimed her ladyship, then mendaciously since she had no memory of having seen these glasses before, added, "They are as lovely as I remember! Thank you, Fotherington!"

"It's my pleasure, my lady," replied the older man, gravely. "I have never served Sauternes in them before, but if that is what your ladyship wishes…"

"Yes, it is! The wine will be even better in such a nice glass. Look how the red glass glows in the candlelight!" In fact, it did look very nice, and once they had both been served Sophy took a small sip. "It's delicious!" she cried. It was true. The wine was cool and sweet. "Lysander, why haven't we had this before?"

For his part, her husband had to fight against a moue of dislike as the wine reached his tongue. Although he was very partial to the sweet course after meals, he had never liked sweet wine. He had only chosen it as it was rarely drunk in the house and the butler would have to search for it. "Er... I'd forgotten we had it. It only came to me just now. I'm glad you like it, my love. We must serve it more often."

He looked at Fotherington, who had served him long enough to be perfectly aware of his taste in wines. The whole evening was puzzling the poor butler more and more, but years of training kept his countenance impassive. "Y... yes, my lord, of course."

He moved to refill her ladyship's glass. Sophy had discovered that the almond pastries and the wine were a perfect combination, and had finished the first glass without realizing it. She accepted the second glass, oblivious to her husband's raised eyebrows.

"You may leave the rest on the table, Fotherington," he said. "We will serve ourselves. And we will be going up directly after dinner. It has been a long day. You may inform Winton and Susan." The butler bowed and left them.

"This wine is perfectly lovely with these tarts and strawberries," said Sophy. "Why don't you have some more?"

"I haven't finished this yet," replied her husband with a smile, "and, though it goes against the grain to tell you, as I would love to be able to take advantage of you in your cups I don't think you should have any more either. Sweet wine gives one a damned awful hangover."

When they were both ready, Sophy rose, swayed a little and gripped the edge of the table. "Goodness, I feel quite dizzy! You are right about that wine. It's dangerous! My goodness!" She giggled. "I think you'd better help me up the stairs!"

Her husband shook his head and smiled. "Hmm... perhaps I shall be able to take advantage of you after all. I hope so! Seriously though," he added, "you must drink a lot of water before going to bed. It will help."

He took her elbow and led her up to her bedchamber, where Susan assisted a more than usually helpless Sophy to disrobe and put away her jewelry. Then she curtseyed and left. Remembering what Lysander had said, Sophy drank two glasses of water, hiccupped and climbed slowly into bed, her head spinning. A few minutes later, her husband returned in his dressing gown.

"Oh dear," she said, "I think I'd better lie here quietly. I'm sorry, Lysander, but I really don't feel at all the thing!"

"And I was going to show you some of those illustrations we were talking about," smiled her husband, indicating a slim volume he held in his hand. "But I'm not surprised. For some reason sweet wine goes to one's head more quickly than anything else. Try to drink more water before you go to sleep."

He kissed her goodnight and went into his own room, leaving the door open, however. Sophy gulped down more water, vowing never to drink alcohol again. But just before she fell asleep, she thought this would be a good way to pass off feeling unwell in the morning.

CHAPTER TWENTY-ONE

In which Sylvester and his Mama take tea

And the next morning feel unwell, she did. She awoke very early, and, as the day before, had to run to vomit in the water closet. Thankfully, her husband appeared not to have heard, so she quietly brushed her teeth and went back to bed. She must have fallen asleep again, because she found herself woken up two hours later by Lysander, who surprised her by being fully dressed.

"I'm sorry to wake you, my love," he said. "I was just going to write you a note. How are you feeling this morning? Head aching, dry mouth, all the classic signs of post intoxication?"

"As a matter of fact, I feel quite well," she retorted. "I was not drunk, just a little tipsy. I am perfectly well now." This was not entirely true, but she felt foolish admitting anything more.

"Hmm," he looked unconvinced, but continued, "I'm sorry, but I had forgotten that today is the horse fair in Chesham. I have to leave early and may not be back until quite late. I told Rogers we would go to buy a pony for Sylvester and one of the carriage horses is developing an odd gait. I noticed it the other day on the trip here. It'll make for a damned uncomfortable ride if it carries on. He really should be replaced. I'll probably have to buy a pair. And perhaps a horse for you?"

Lysander knew she did not really want to ride; she had told him so in as many words a number of times, but he never gave up. So she just put her arms up for a kiss and said only, "Well, I shall miss you, but have a lovely day and don't smile at all the ladies and break their hearts."

"I only smile at one lady and she is more likely to break *my* heart," he said, coming into her arms and kissing her. "I had such plans for last night, with Sylvester sound asleep and the whole evening before us. But..."

"I'm sorry," replied his wife. "I promise to do better tonight. Please don't buy a horse for me and make sure the one you get for Sylvester is really docile!"

"Don't worry, my love," he said, leaving her. "We won't get anything our son can't handle. Though for some reason, I think we shall find he can handle just about anything."

"Are you by chance going to visit your grandmother today?" she asked Susan sometime later, when her maid was dealing with her unruly curls. "I would like to meet her. I expect she knows all sorts of things about the old days and can tell some interesting tales."

"Oh, Mum and Gran would love it if you come to tea!" exclaimed Susan. "If you give me leave, I'll run 'ome and tell me Mum you're coming. They're there all the time, but Mum would want to tidy up, like, and get 'erself ready before you arrive."

"Oh dear, I don't want to give her any trouble. I wish she wouldn't do anything special."

"Me lady, she will be so 'appy to have you to tea, you can't imagine! And not tidy up? Never, in a month of Sundays!"

"Well, if you're sure, I'll come about four o'clock. I'll bring Sylvester with me. He will keep us all amused!"

So it was that later that afternoon her ladyship and her son who, much to his disgust, had been washed and changed for the outing, set out for Susan's home. Sophy had decided the walk would do them both good, but had ordered the carriage for their return at half past five. Susan accompanied them, showing them a shortcut across the fields which involved climbing over a stile, to the great amusement of the young lord. He went back and forth across it finding ever more ingenious ways to do so, at one point threatening to go underneath. He was prevented from doing so by his mother who could only envisage the muddy child who would emerge. The rest of the time he spent looking for rats in the stalks of oats, but though rats there certainly were, none of them was inclined to meet the young master.

They arrived at the farm and, after a deep curtsey, were ushered into the rarely-used parlor by Susan's delighted mother. This lady regarded Sophy as something of a saint, since she had elevated her daughter from downstairs maid to lady's maid, with all its attendant honors. By now, Susan had several working gowns and two or three pretty dresses made specially for her by her ladyship's own *modiste*; she sat at the servant's table only one place below the butler and was afforded the respect due to her status, including being referred to by her last name. For her mother this was an unending source of pride, and if she sometimes lorded it over her less fortunate neighbors, it was only to be expected.

Her ladyship was introduced to Susan's grandmother, a woman crippled by rheumatism, who nevertheless tried to rise to greet her. Sophy took her hand and urged her to remain seated.

The old lady, retaining a grip on her hand, gazed into her eyes with a piercing look and said, in a reedy but strong voice, "It's a girl you're carrying, me lady. A bonny girl. I can see her."

"Oh!" said Sophy, hardly knowing how to respond. She had only just realized her condition herself and was amazed that Susan's grandmother could know it.

"Now, Gran, don't be imagining things," rebuked Susan's mother. "I'm sorry, me lady, Gran does 'ave her funny ways."

"Oh, but..." Sophy decided to tell the truth. "She's right about my carrying a child. I believe I am, but please don't tell anyone. I haven't said anything to his lordship. I think it better to wait three months to avoid disappointment."

"There won't be no disappointment, me lady," came grandmother's reedy voice. "She's well 'ooked in, that one. There'll be no losing her."

"What wunnerful news, me lady!" cried Susan. "But all the maternity clothes is in London. Whatever shall we do? I'll just 'ave to invent a reason for 'is lordship to let me take a carriage down there!"

"We have time," said Sophy. "No need to worry about it now."

Sylvester, bored by all this woman talk, had meanwhile wondered over to the hearth where a large sandy-colored dog of indeterminate breed lay snoozing. He hesitated, then patted the dog on its big square head. The dog opened one eye and obligingly rolled over for a tummy rub. The boy willingly co-operated and they were well on the way to becoming fast friends when he was called to wash his hands for tea.

A tea table had been set on one side of the parlor. It bore a snowy cloth, embroidered with flowers around the edges and in the center.

"Gran made this years ago," said Susan, "before her rheumatics got so bad. She used to be wunnerful with a needle."

"That must be where you inherit it from," said Sophy, for Susan was herself a very good seamstress. "I wish I could sew! This tablecloth is so pretty!"

"But your paintings is lovely, me lady," said Susan's mother. "Look what our Susie give me!"

Sophy looked where she was pointing and saw that the tulip painting she had given her maid was hung in pride of place above the chimney.

"I recall," said Susan's grandmother suddenly, "my old Granny telling me that they ate flower bulbs in the winter when they was 'ungry and 'ad nothin' else. Back over a hunnerd years ago, that must 'ave been. She didn't come from 'ere, mind. From the north somewhere she was."

As the bread and butter was passed around, the fruitcake sliced and the tea sipped, there was a general conversation about plants that could be eaten. Dandelion leaves were, of course, good for salads, so long as you picked them before the flower appeared, as that made them bitter. But Sophy learned that the countryfolk also ate clover, chickweed, dock and, to her surprise, cattails. "The roots and the young leaves taste a bit like onions," said Susan's mother, "and you can roast the young cattail itself."

Sylvester's eyes grew big and round. "Roast the cat's tail? You a bad lady! I yunge you with my sword if you roast my kitty's tail!"

There was an immediate outcry of four voices at once. From Susan: "Not a real kitty, master Sylvester! It's a plant!" From her mother: "Oh, the poor child! I didn't mean that!" From Sophy: "Sylvester! You mustn't talk about killing people with your sword. He didn't mean it. It's only a toy!" And from grandmother a loud cackle: "That's the way, me young lord! You tell 'em!"

Once the hubbub had died down and Sylvester had understood what they were talking about, Sophy said that if he had finished he might be excused, but to remember his manners and say 'thank you' to Susan's Mama. This was accomplished very prettily, for the boy was constantly being groomed on his manners both by his mother and his father. Their hostess having declared him a lovely little boy, he removed himself back to the hearth and the dog.

Susan told him that Major would, if asked, give him his paw, and bring back a stick if you threw it for him, but not inside, mind. Sylvester happily amused himself while the ladies talked. He was delighted with the paw trick for a while, and then decided to go outside to throw a stick for the dog, who obligingly brought it back. This was a fine game and would have continued, had not Major spied a rabbit at the end of the garden where the family grew vegetables, and given immediate chase. The dog ran after the rabbit and the boy ran after the dog, who soon disappeared into the trees at the far end of the property. Sylvester knew better than to wander into the woods on his own, and returned towards the cottage smacking at bushes and fences with the dog's stick.

Inside the cottage, the clock on the mantlepiece, a Christmas present from Susan to her father after her second year of employment as a lady's maid, chimed the half hour. Sophy realized with a start that the carriage would already be there to pick them up. How the time had flown! She thanked her hostesses for the lovely tea and congratulated them on the fruitcake, which, she said, was better than the one at the Court, but please not to mention she had said so! Stepping outside, she was surprised not to see Sylvester with the dog, who had by now returned from his unsuccessful chase. She looked around and called his name, not really worried. He knew not to wander off.

Susan and her mother had come out with her ladyship. Her maid said, "He may be out back at the privy. I'll go and see." In a few moments she was back, shaking her head.

"Where can he have gone?" wondered Sophy, looking intently at the dog, who, though he knew, was incapable of telling.

She suddenly had an idea. "Is there a pond nearby?" She was thinking of the boating experiments and convinced herself that he would be there. Susan and she both ran to the water's edge, but there was no sign of him. Then an awful thought struck her. Could he have waded in and... drowned? Her heart stopped and she had to dig her nails into her palms not to cry out.

"Susan," she said with deadly calm, "will you run and ask your brothers to wade through the pond with long poles – pitchforks or something?" Susan's brothers were in the fields with their father. They had passed them on their walk.

As her maid left, her face as white as her lace collar, Sophy walked swiftly to the carriage and instructed the groom to walk the horses slowly up the lane and back, looking carefully in all the ditches on both sides. "Sylvester is missing" was all she said. The groom nodded, said nothing and, his face set, immediately did as he was bid.

It was not long before all the farmers and labourers in the vicinity knew what had happened. The same fleet-footed children who had warned of their coming the previous day now ran with the message that the young master had disappeared. Every man dropped his tools where he stood and side by side lines were formed, walking at arms' lengths through the fields, hoping to find him and dreading to do so. Nothing. Susan's brothers probed the pond. Nothing. Susan, her youngest brother and her mother went into the woods at the end of the garden calling Sylvester's name. Nothing.

At her wits' end and steeling herself not to break down, longing for her husband to return and take charge, Sophy wondered what to do next. When the groom returned from a fruitless search of the hedgerows, she told him to unhitch the horses from the carriage, take one and gallop to the Court. Ask Rogers – no, he had gone with Lysander – ask the grooms to saddle as many horses as there were men to ride them, and go down all the roads and paths while there was still enough light to see. She would stay where she was, in case her son somehow found his way back to where he had started. She walked around the farmhouse again, trembling, determined not to cry, looking in every corner, probing the bottom of the water butt with a long branch, calling and calling till her voice was hoarse. It was now past seven and the sun would set in less than an hour.

Where was Lysander? Surely he must be home by now! She was desperate for the sound of his voice when suddenly, she heard it calling her. She hurried back to the front of the farmhouse and saw him. He was astride Caesar, his huge black stallion, and truly looked as if he could command anything and anyone. When he saw her, he came towards her, and, as he had done four years ago, when they were first married, lifted her with one arm and settled her, sidesaddle, in front of him.

She pressed her head against his shoulder and gave way. Her voice broke, and with a shuddering sob she cried, "I've done everything I can think of, Lysander. Where can he be? He hasn't fallen into the pond, or into a ditch. He isn't in the fields or the woods. He's nowhere to be found!" She raised her head with a wail, "It's my fault! I wasn't watching him! He was playing with the dog and then he was gone! Oh, Lysander, it's all my fault!"

He dropped both the reins and held her tight. "It does no good to think that way. It's not a question of who's at fault, and I'm sure you are not. You kept your head. I'm proud of you. Fotherington tells me you gave the order for all the horses to be taken by anyone who could ride to search all the highways and byways. That is exactly what I would have done. You have looked everywhere you could look and had the pond probed. That is what I would have done, too. You have done everything anyone could have done. Sylvester will be found. He will be filthy dirty and talking his head off about swords and rats, but he will be found. Everyone on the estate is looking for him. He will be found. Now, let me take you home."

The sun had almost set by the time they got back to the Court. The old bricks and vines were half in shadow and half bathed in the last rays of golden light. The roses perfumed the air with their delicious scent. But husband and wife noticed none of it. As they entered the huge oak door, the women servants were waiting silently in the great hall with Fotherington. All the men who could had ridden off to look for the child. The women surged forward for news. Lysander shook his head and the butler urged them back to their duties, saying it was no good them all standing around doing nothing. His lordship helped Sophy into the blue parlor. She was speechless, shaking with fear and despair. He gave orders for tea and sandwiches.

"I'm going to ride around one last time while there's still a little light. Please try to eat and drink something. It will make you feel better. I won't be gone long."

She wanted him to stay and she wanted him to go. She wanted to go outside and run in every direction at once, but she knew it was useless. She sat down and wept. The tea went cold and the edges of the sandwiches curled.

Lysander returned about an hour later, by which time it was completely dark. He tried to hide his grim expression from his wife and sought to cheer her by recounting the times when Sylvester had run away from his disagreeable Nannies, to be found hours later asleep under a bed or curled in a corner somewhere.

"I am sure that is what has happened," said Lysander, holding his trembling wife tightly in his arms. "He fell asleep and apart from being hungry and perhaps a little fearful, he is perfectly all right. No one hereabouts would harm a hair on his head, and he is a courageous little man. We will continue the search in the morning and he will be found, demanding almond tarts and muffins."

He kissed her cheek and tried to look more cheerful than he felt. Neither of them could bear to think, much less talk, about their little boy crying and afraid in the dark.

CHAPTER TWENTY-TWO

In which Sylvester has good manners

His lordship was quite right, of course. As Sylvester was returning to the cottage, a little disconsolate at the disappearance of his dog playmate, the group of gypsies he had met the day before passed by on the path outside the garden gate. The long line of carts and homes on wheels had started late because of problems with one of the wheels on Petrin's *vardo*. The same wheel chose that moment to give a suspicious wobble, and at the head of the line, Petrin reined in. The last cart drew to a halt just outside the gate where Sylvester now stood. It was a simple arrangement with hoops covered by a canvas from side to side and rolled down behind the driver. It was used to carry hay for the horses and other supplies.

Sylvester remembered his father's words about wanting to roll along with the gypsies, and it seemed a good idea to him too. He slipped out of the gate and in an instant was up into the cart, lying on a bed of hay, his feet towards the front and his head at the back opening, from where he could see the sky and interestingly shaped clouds. He and Daisy would often play a game of trying to find things they recognized in the clouds. As he looked at the blue and white heavens, the cart suddenly jolted into movement and set off at a sedate pace along the path. In no wise perturbed, the young lord continued staring at the sky, his head pillowed on the fragrant hay, his body rocked by the swaying of the cart, and it was not long before he was fast asleep.

He remained so until the cart drew to a halt, the rocking stopped and the night air began to be a little chilly. By that time the troupe had been traveling about three hours and were some twelve miles from the village of Hale, heading south, where they would find work berry picking. The gypsies had been traveling these paths for generations and rarely went by the king's highway. There were tolls to be paid and hamlets to be passed through that they preferred to avoid. While they were, by and large, a law-abiding group, they were always blamed for anything that went awry during their passage, from fire and theft to a miscarriage or a baby born with a hare-lip. So they rolled along uninhabited lanes, along fields and through woodland that had been trod by the people of this part of the world since Roman times, but which figured on no map. It was therefore not surprising that no one from the many search groups saw them.

His lordship was also correct about his son's frame of mind. When Sylvester awoke, he was conscious only of being very hungry. He was not afraid. He knew he was in a gypsy cart and he knew that Petrin was his father's friend. As a lucky child who had never gone hungry or had an enemy in his life, he had no doubt that someone would feed him, so it was with absolute assurance that he scrambled down from the cart.

The first thing the Romany women and children always did when setting up camp was to build a fire and it was towards that flickering light that he walked. At first, no one noticed him, a small, shadowy figure among many others. But as he came into the full light of the fire and the flames shone on his curly chestnut locks, the women fell back, speechless, as if before an apparition. Then Petrin's wife, who had embraced Sylvester so warmly the day before, saw him and, crying out loudly in her own language, held out her arms towards him. The lessons his Papa had taught him came as if by instinct, and he bowed, pronouncing his usual formula, "'Vester Barrington, 'tyour service."

Petrin heard his wife's loud exclamation and came running. He stared in amazement at Sylvester, who came forward, holding out his little hand as Fotherington had taught him. "G'evning Petrin! I tust find you well," he said, adding after a slight pause, "and baby Danior."

The women in the group understood nothing of this except the word *Danior*, and stood stunned by the amazing sight of this child apparition, surely no more than three or four years old, greeting their leader with an outstretched hand. To escape the babble of interrogatory voices that then broke out, Petrin led the young lord to one side and with some difficulty finally understood from him what had happened.

"... and now I's most fearfl'y hungry. I missed my supper, I specks," concluded Sylvester.

"Then you eat fast and I take you home," said Petrin, and shouted an order to the women.

The group had eaten a stew of root vegetables and hedgehog at lunch time, and there was some left. It was quickly warmed up and given to Sylvester with a chunk of bread. Like his Papa, he was not fond of vegetables and the meat was a mystery to him, but breeding will out. He ate the dish stoically, and even quite enjoyed it when one of the older matrons showed him how to break the rather stale bread into the gravy. He was wise enough not to ask for a sweet course, though his mind dwelt longingly on the almond tarts at home. He remembered to thank them politely for the meal, and they answered in their own way. Neither side understood the words of the other, but the meaning was clear.

In the meantime, Petrin had saddled up the only horse they possessed capable of returning, and swiftly, the twelve miles it had just walked. He mounted the horse, a stocky piebald cob, and had Sylvester handed up in front of him. He took a wide leather belt and pulled it tight around himself and the boy, then, as his father had done in the park that day, fastened his coat with Sylvester inside, with just his head sticking out.

"Now lookee, young master," he said, "we've got to get you home before your poor mother worrits herself to death. Please to lean back into me and don't move about!"

It was the ride of Sylvester's life. How many times had he begged his father to gallop, and how many times been refused. He rejoiced now as they set off at as fast a pace as Petrin thought the horse could manage, down the long side of a field. He was disappointed when they had to slow to a trot in the woods, but his heart leaped as they went into a canter and back to a short gallop again.

He proved to be a natural rider. He allowed his body to melt into the gait of the horse, and he was fearless. In this way they rode the miles back to Hale Court. Petrin tried to save his horse as much as he could, but he knew that speed was vital. Would he walk or trot his horse if Danior was missing? They covered the twelve miles in something over an hour, dashed at full tilt under the brick arch, wheeled around the wide gravel path and drew up in a shower of stones before the front door.

Fotherington, who for hours had been anxiously peering outside every ten minutes, heard the galloping approach and threw open the front door. Panting, Petrin undid his coat and the leather belt and handed down the boy.

He was no sooner on his feet than Sylvester ran into the hall, stumbling a little as his legs readjusted to being upright, shouting at the top of his voice, "Mama! Papa! I galloped! I galloped all the way! I like galloping!" In the excitement no one noticed he had finally learned to pronounce his L's.

The Earl and his Lady were sitting quietly in the blue parlor, his arms around her, there being no words left for either of them to say. When they heard the familiar voice, they started up. Sophy did not wait for her husband. She ran into the hall and dropped to her knees to gather the running figure into her arms, crying and laughing at once and holding him as if to hold him for ever. His lordship stopped only long enough to drop a kiss on his son's head and whisper "Thank God!" before striding to the front door and holding out his hand to Petrin.

Sylvester quickly tired of being clutched to his mother's breast and ran to where his father and the gypsy were talking, Petrin explaining what had happened.

"Papa! I galloped! Din't I, Petrin? I very liked it!" and he careered around the hall in his own version of the gallop.

By now the rest of the household had heard of the young lord's safe return and crowded into the hall. Daisy came running in and caught him in mid gallop to give him a hug and a kiss. "I knew you wasn't really lost, Sylvester," she said. "You're too clever for that! Where've you been?"

"Yes, tell me too," said his Mama, sitting on the floor in the middle of the hall. Daisy sat down with her and Sylvester explained in his own way what had happened.

"Major dog runned away an' I seed the cart an' I rolled with the gypsies like Papa said an' I seed clouds in the sky and I went to seep an' I woked up and the lady gived me vegebles and gravy and I eated it but I didn't like it and I said thank you and Petrin galloped me home an' can I gallop 'gain 'morrow, Mama, can I?"

Sophy understood her son perfectly, as mothers always do, and answered that he would have to speak to Papa about galloping, "But please don't climb into carts any more, Sylvester, at least, not without telling someone, because Mama and Papa were *so worried* when we didn't know where you were. And did you say thank you to Petrin for bringing you home?"

The boy scrambled to his feet and ran over to his Papa and Petrin. "Thank you, Petrin, for galloping me! I liked it *so much*! Papa! Can I gallop again 'morrow? Pleese?" He turned his wide blue eyes on his father.

"No need to thank, young master." replied Petrin, "Very good to us always, the Hales." Turning to the Earl he added, "Got a good seat for a horse, he has, me lord. Rode like he was born to it. Talk of riding, I have to ask you to lend me a horse for returning. Old Molly, she's fair knackered. No way can the poor old girl make it back. May have to be put down."

"Just a minute, Sylvester," said his lordship to his son who was tugging his hand. "Let me talk to Petrin." He turned to their saviour. "I won't *lend* you a horse, my friend, I'll *give* you one. Matter of fact I'm just back from the horse fair in Chesham and I bought a nice working bay. She's got good Welsh stock in her – strong legs and a small head. Take her with my thanks, Petrin, take her. She's yours to use, sell or trade, as you wish. Leave Molly here and we'll save her if we can. She deserves it."

The Romany was not comfortable taking anything from his lordship and needed some persuasion, but finally agreed. Sophy asked if he'd missed his supper, and finding that he had, took him downstairs where Mrs. Simmons gave him what was probably the best meal of his life. Like the rest of the household, she could not do enough for the man who had brought back the young master.

His lordship was able then to assure his importunate son that yes, they would gallop the next day and, moreover, he would have his first lesson on his new pony. The ecstatic boy was also taken downstairs for almond tarts, which he generously shared with Petrin, and then his Mama took him up for his bath, still talking.

The Earl went into his study and composed the following letter, to which he affixed his seal of hot wax with the H signet ring impressed into it.

Hale Court, Buckinghamshire

To whom it may concern:

Let it be known that the bearer of this letter is owed a great debt by the Hale Family. As a consequence, Petrin Codon, his offspring and extended family, are to be afforded every consideration wherever the name of Hale be known and respected.

Signed this 28th day of May, in the year of our Lord 1820.

Lysander Barrington, Fifth Earl of Hale

He went downstairs to the kitchen where Petrin had finished his meal and was leaning back in his chair, wondering if he could smoke.

"Come into my study for a cigar and a brandy," he said to the Romany, "before you get on your way. I know I could do with it."

The visitor willingly agreed and when they were settled, the Earl gave him the letter. Petrin looked at it for a moment and then said with an apology in his voice, "I can do letters well enough when needed, me lord, but I'd be obliged if you'd read me what it says."

His lordship readily did so, and handed it back. Petrin folded it reverently and put it in his pocket. He was to take it out later and tell, rather than read, its contents to his family. This, together with the present of the fine horse, not to mention the apparition of the young master out of the shadows, marked the day as a very special one in their calendar. It was a story to be told over and over for many years to come. Indeed, you may still hear it today if you travel long enough in those parts.

Petrin took his leave not long after, anxious to get back to his wife and family. The bay Lysander had given him proved very fine indeed and he made the trip back in under an hour. His lordship made his way upstairs to the nursery, where Sylvester was already in bed and almost asleep.

"Papa!" he murmured, "I see my pony 'morrow. I call him Danior."

"Well, perhaps Danny would be better. Petrin will certainly think his son is more important than a pony. I know I do." He kissed his son fondly. "I never doubted you, my boy," he added, under his breath.

"Danny. Thass a nice name," agreed Sylvester, then he was asleep.

Lysander and Sophy walked arm in arm to their rooms.

"You smell of cigars," remarked Sophy, whose stomach had lurched when the scent met her nostrils.

"Yes, I had one to keep Petrin company. What a good man he is. Salt of the earth. And to think that some people mistrust the Romanys. No one on the Hale estate will ever do so again, I promise you."

"Good," said Sophy and hastened her steps. She ran into her room and immediately to the water closet, where she was violently sick.

Thinking her reaction was the result of overstrung nerves, her husband gently rubbed her back as she knelt over the commode, and soothed her anxiously. "Hush. It's over now, my love. He's home. Hush!"

Sophy looked up from her inglorious position and smiled. "It's not that! I can tell you now. I'm increasing, Lysander. I'm expecting a child! I think it's from the night of the piano... you know. Something wonderful came out of that awful time. You are going to be a Papa to a little girl, according to Susan's grandmother. Imagine that! A little girl. May we call her Margaret, after my mother?"

"And Alice, after mine," he replied with his wonderful smile, pulling her up into his arms. "Margaret Alice. And she will be as beautiful and kind as her mother. Thank you, my love, thank you."

Margaret Alice did indeed grow up to be as beautiful as her mother. But in the mysterious ways that family resemblances work, she looked more like her father, though happily without the Hale nose. She had her mother's porcelain skin and her lovely figure, but her Papa's almost black wavy hair, deep brown eyes and fine eyebrows. Quite unlike her brother, she was a scholar. His Papa always maintained Sylvester could have been sired by his uncle Charles, so great was his affinity for sport, especially riding. Lysander taught Margaret to play the piano and read Latin and Greek. In her late twenties, she was one of the supporters of the Ladies College in Bedford

Square, the first college for women in the country. She taught the classics. She was everywhere liked and admired. Her father adored her. He very *yiked* her, he said, even better than roast beef, even better than *Fino* and yes, even better than trifle.

THE END

If you enjoyed this story, please leave a review on Amazon. Just scroll down the book page and click in the appropriate spot. This is the link:

https://www.amazon.com/Earl-Heir-House-Hale-Three-ebook/dp/B08LDFHN59/ref=sr

The Earl and the Heir is the third book in the House of Hale series. If you'd like to see the beginning of the saga, these are the links:

Book One: *The Earl and The Mud-Covered Maiden*
https://www.amazon.com/Earl-Mud-Covered-Maiden-House-Hale-ebook/dp/B08CTKX8KM/ref=sr

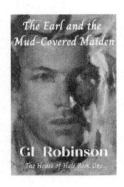

Book Two: The Earl and His Lady
https://www.amazon.com/Earl-his-Lady-House-Hale-ebook/dp/B08GL3H753/ref=sr

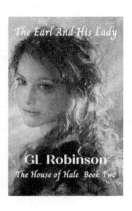

My other Regency Romances are available on Amazon.

Imogen or Love and Money. Wealthy and beautiful young widow Imogen thinks she will find happiness investing her late husband's fortune. She does, but what then?
https://www.amazon.com/Imogen-Love-Money-Regency-Romance-ebook/dp/B07ZXKVSNY/ref=sr

Cecilia or Too Tall to Love. Orphaned Cecilia, too tall and too outspoken for acceptance by the *ton,* is determined to open a school for girls in London's East End slums, but is lacking funds. When Lord Tommy Allenby offers her a way out, will she get more than she bargained for?
https://www.amazon.com/Cecilia-Too-Tall-Love-Regency-ebook/dp/B084DXNNYX/ref=sr

Rosemary or Too Clever to Love. Governess Rosemary is forced to move with her pupil, the romantically-minded Marianne, to live with the girl's guardian, a strict gentleman with old fashioned ideas about young women should behave. Can she save the one from her own folly and persuade the other that she isn't just a not-so-pretty face?
https://www.amazon.com/Rosemary-Too-Clever-Love-Regency-ebook/dp/B086N3B88V/ref=sr

The Kissing Ball. A Collection of Short Stories. An unexpected Christmas guest finds love, but not where she expects it; a middle-aged widowed gentlewoman is surprised when an unusual new neighbor turns up looking for help; a young woman finds a buyer for her father's chemistry laboratory, but gets more than she bargained for; Sir Robert befriends a homely governess and his future is changed forever by a dog and a dimple; a young woman with an extraordinarily beautiful best friend discovers that she isn't necessarily cast into the shade. Then in present-day London, Ginny finds out her new next-door neighbor is not quite what she expected.

https://www.amazon.com/Kissing-Ball-Christmas-Regency-Stories-ebook/dp/B08LDZZ7NX/ref=sr

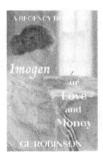  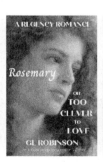 

Please leave reviews and feel free to contact me. I love to hear from my readers!

https://romancenovelsbyglrobinson.com

About the Author

GL Robinson was born and educated in the south of England, but has lived for over forty years in the USA with her American husband. She tried and failed to adopt an American accent, so people still call her The English Lady! She is a retired French professor, and loves flowers in the garden, eating with friends and talking with her grandchildren. She has published two children's travel books for ages 8-11 inspired by one of them.

She was inspired to start writing after the unexpected death of her dear sister in July 2018. They were educated in a convent boarding school and would giggle at historical Romances after lights-out under the covers. They were, and are, a life-long passion for them both. All her Regency Romances are dedicated to her sister.

The House of Hale trilogy was the result of thinking about what might happen *after* the wedding, which is where Regency Romances usually end!

For more information about the author, to listen to her read from her books, receive a free short story, or get sneak previews about upcoming books, please go to:

https://romancenovelsbyglrobinson.com

Printed in Great Britain
by Amazon